Playing Away

Playing Away

CARYL PHILLIPS

faber and faber

LONDON · BOSTON

In association with
Channel Four Television Company Ltd

First published in 1987 by
Faber and Faber Limited
3 Queen Square London WCIN 3AU

Filmset by Wilmaset Birkenhead Wirral
Printed in Great Britain by
Redwood Burn Ltd Trowbridge Wiltshire
All rights reserved

British Library Cataloguing in Publication Data

Phillips, Caryl
Playing away.
I. Title
822'.914   PR6066.H45/

ISBN 0–571–14583–3

For Frances

Introduction

It is a fact that most West Indian migrants came from a predominantly rural background to work in cold urban Britain. Their knowledge of traffic jams, fog, smog, pubs, and factory floors was limited, if it existed at all. Days of toil close to the soil characterized the lifestyles of those of the African diaspora who ended up in the Caribbean. For the pioneer generation who emigrated to England, the transition from a warm and open lifestyle to a closed concrete and glass one was both harsh and swift. Their children have subsequently grown up in this urban environment, and in today's Britain it is true to say that the vast majority of West Indians and Black Britons continue to live in the city.

Yet, despite her claim to fame as the mother of industrialization, Britain is still a society with a country gentry, and an agricultural class committed to the land. Industrial Britain has by no means devoured all the fair hills and green pastures. Many of the shapers of British attitudes are still to be found in the country estates of the Home Counties, their wealth closeted well away from back-to-back terraced streets, their lives reasonably independent from the often drab rituals of the city.

My parents were of that first pioneer generation, and they introduced me to the industrial forests of Leeds and Birmingham where trees belonged in parks. As I grew older, and went to university, I became aware of another face to Britain. Some of my new friends lived on estates. Not the council estates of my youth, but forty to fifty-acre spreads with streams and little bridges. Others, of more modest origin, simply lived in villages where the idea of choosing between the Mecca and the Odeon for a night's entertainment was out of the question. There was a pub. They went to it or they stayed at home and watched television or read a book.

In order to dramatize my 'discovery' I thought about using a university setting, but it smacked too uncomfortably of an autobiographical sketch that I preferred not to draw. I would have to approach the subject more obliquely. The 'facts' were that, in the main, West Indians and Black Britons lived and worked in the city. Britons who were unused to the city would, by implication, be unused to West Indians and Black Britons. In order that they might come together they needed to share something innocent, such as a game. Cricket, for instance, a love they both have in common. Having decided this, there was only one more decision I had to make before putting pen to paper. Which one of the teams would play away? It was easy. The team that had been playing away the longest.

Caryl Phillips
LONDON May 1986

The film, *Playing Away*, was made for Channel Four by Insight Productions. It was first shown at the London Film Festival in November 1986. The cast was as follows:

SANDRA	Liz Anson
KEVIN	Mark Barratt
ERROL	Gary Beadle
WILLIE BOY	Norman Beaton
STUART	Brian Bovell
PAT	Valerie Buchanan
DAVID	Ian Cross
JOHN	Larry Dann
MISS RYE	Zulema Dene
DEREK	Nicholas Farrell
BOOTS	Jim Findley
MICK	Julian Granger
WILF	Ram John Holder
COLONEL	Patrick Holt
LOUIS	Stefan Kalipha
SONNY	Ross Kemp
TOMMY	Gareth Kirkland
WEST INDIAN WOMAN	Lucita Lijertwood
MARJORIE	Helen Lindsay
YVETTE	Suzette Llewellyn
ROBBO	Joseph Marcell
STEADROY	Archie Pool
VICAR	Roddy Maude-Roxby
IAN	Neil Morrisey
CONSTABLE	Charles Pemberton
FREDRICK	Bruce Purchase
TAVERN BARMAN	Jimmy Reddington
VIV	Sheila Ruskin
DESERT HEAD	Errol Shaker
MASIE	Femi Taylor

ANGIE	Mary Tempest
JEFF	Trevor Thomas
GODFREY	Robert Urquhart
JULIE	Juliet Waley

Crew:

Script Editor	Peter Ansorge
Lighting Cameraman	Nic Knowland
Art Director	Pip Gardner
Music Director	Simon Webb
Editor	Graham Whitlock
Associate Producer	Chris Sutton
Producers	Vijay Amarnani and Brian Skilton
Director	Horace Ové

EXT. SNEDDINGTON. EVENING.
We establish the picturesque English village of Sneddington. The birds are singing. Friday evening. Peace. Harmony.

EXT. BRIXTON STREET. EVENING.
WILLIE BOY *stands outside a phone box. He is in his late forties but dresses a little younger. He carries a rolled-up copy of a daily tabloid. Inside the phone box is a fat middle-aged (forty-ish)* WEST INDIAN WOMAN. WILLIE BOY *is at the head of a short queue. He looks at his watch and fidgets. (*WOMAN *wears M & S type skirt, top and cardigan and carries two plastic carrier-bags full of groceries.)*

EXT. VILLAGE. EVENING.
Wide shot above village hall showing roofs of houses around the village hall, and fields in the background. Camera cranes down and holds in front of the hall.

INT. VILLAGE HALL. EVENING.
DEREK *and* VIV *sit together.* DEREK *is about thirty-five, a banker, dressed casually in trousers and short-sleeved, open-necked shirt (looks like Austin Reed but is from Burton) as this is the weekend.* VIV, *his wife, is thirty. She has on a soft, flowery dress and flat pumps. She looks slightly uneasy. We hear* MARJORIE'S *voice. She is in her late fifties.*
MARJORIE: A safari was something we both looked forward to.
　　(DEREK *looks at his watch.* VIV *gives him a reprimanding glance. We hear the rattle of a slide carousel.*
　　DEREK *looks apologetically at* VIV *and moves to get up. In same shot we see the rest of the audience, about twenty sitting in rows of chairs.*
　　MARJORIE *stands by the slide projector. It is her voice we heard. She is well-dressed, in twin set and pearls, gold spectacles. She reads from notes.*
　　From MARJORIE'S *POV we see* DEREK *getting up as his shadow passes across the screen.*

I

MARJORIE *looks disapprovingly at* DEREK's *move.*)
As you can see it wasn't all play.

EXT.   BRIXTON STREET.   EVENING.
Outside the phone box. Again WILLIE BOY *looks at his watch.
Then his patience snaps. He opens the door to the phone box but the*
WOMAN *carries on her conversation.*
WILLIE BOY: Jesus, I have an emergency case! A 999 call!
      (*The* WOMAN *pushes him out of the box.*)

EXT.   VILLAGE SQUARE.   EVENING.
*In the square there is a pub, the hall, a war memorial, small cottage,
shops, etc.*
Three local lads, IAN, MICK *and* SONNY *stand by a red Ford
Escort.* IAN *has hair cut short on sides, a bit spiky on top and
long in back. The other two have similar styles – country boys
trying to imitate the latest London look. All three wear a 'tough'
look style.*
They look across at the hall.
SONNY: What's going on in there?
IAN: A slide show. Penultimate event.
SONNY: Fancy going?
      (MICK *and* IAN *look at him with contempt.* SONNY *looks
      slightly embarrassed.*)

INT.   ANTE-ROOM IN VILLAGE HALL.   EVENING.
DEREK *is holding open an address book with one hand and dialling
a number with the other.*

EXT.   BRIXTON STREET.   EVENING.
WILLIE BOY *is now waiting in the phone box. A* PUNK ROCKER
opens the door to the box. WILLIE BOY *speaks before he can say
anything.*
WILLIE BOY: Listen, my mother's dying. Show some damn
      respect!
      (*The* PUNK *simply stares at him. Then the phone rings.*
      WILLIE BOY *spins around quickly and picks it up. He fumbles
      with the receiver then gets a firm grip on it.*)

2

WILLIE BOY: Yes . . . yes, speaking . . . everything okay? . . .
you sure? . . . about lunchtime . . .

INT.   ANTE-ROOM IN VILLAGE HALL.   EVENING.
DEREK: Fine. Plenty of time to relax. Just a nice little friendly,
eh?

EXT.   BRIXTON STREET.   EVENING.
WILLIE BOY: Just a what? . . . a friendly, . . . okay then . . .
sure . . . we check you later.

EXT.   OUTSIDE A BYRE.   EVENING.
FREDRICK *and his two sons,* TOMMY *and* DAVID, *are herding in the
cows for milking.* FREDRICK *is a local tenant farmer; fifty, broad,
wellington boots and flat cap (maybe wears beat-up tweed jacket).*
DAVID *has crew-cut ginger hair. Sons are in late teens and don't drink
alcohol. One cow won't get in.* FREDRICK *kicks it up the backside.*
FREDRICK: Get in there, you lazy bugger!
(*The sons look at each other.* TOMMY, *the older one, looks at his
watch.*)
TOMMY: Come on, Dad, you could have had two pints by now!
(FREDRICK *wipes his hands down the front of his coat. He
scrapes some dirt off his boots.*)
FREDRICK: I'll not be long.

INT.   VILLAGE HALL.   EVENING.
The blinds are pulled up and the early evening light comes in.
MARJORIE *blinks at the sudden brightness. There is enthusiastic
applause. She smiles at* GODFREY.
Cut to:
GODFREY *sitting in the front row, a black Labrador at his feet. We
recognize him as the colonial gentleman in the slide. He is older now,
in his mid-sixties.*
Cut to:
The VICAR, *a lean man in his forties, as he rises and stands beside*
MARJORIE.
VICAR: Fascinating. Now I'm sure some of you have questions to
ask of Mrs Matthews, so I'll just step aside for a moment.

3

Cut to:
Audience. Pause. It becomes clear that nobody is in a hurry to ask anything.

EXT. BRIXTON STREET. EVENING.
WILLIE BOY *is walking from his flat in Coldharbour Lane past the anti-nuclear mural and goes under the railway bridge. He is approaching traffic lights at Atlantic Road crossroads on his way to the pub.*
Cut to:
Five-year-old BMW speeding up behind WILLIE BOY *approaching same traffic lights. Without looking* WILLIE BOY *goes to cross road to pub. He steps out and BMW swerves, blasts its horn, and passes by, having nearly knocked him down.*
WILLIE BOY: You little fucker. Why you don't watch where you're going?
  (*He stands and looks after it. It glides almost arrogantly away. People in the street stop and check what has happened.*)

INT/EXT. BMW. EVENING.
ERROL *is driving. He is in his early twenties. He has a strong face. He is full of confidence. He looks in his rear-view mirror and laughs at* WILLIE BOY. YVETTE *leans forward and turns down the music from the cassette player. She is twenty-one. Quietly pretty. She looks across at* ERROL.
YVETTE: You nearly knocked my dad down.
ERROL: He shouldn't jump out in front of cars then, should he.
  (YVETTE *looks angrily at him.* ERROL *begins to slow down.*)

EXT. KELLETT STREET – OUTSIDE EFFRA HALL TAVERN ON CORNER OF RATTRAY ROAD. EVENING.
STUART *is standing by the side of the road. He is about Errol's age. He is neatly dressed and wears glasses. He sees the car indicator lights flash on and the car pulling over towards him. The car comes to a halt next to* STUART.

INT. BMW. EVENING.
ERROL *looks across at* YVETTE.

4

ERROL: I don't know what you're looking at me like that for.
(STUART *taps on the side window asking to be let in. As*
ERROL *leans back to open the door* YVETTE *gathers up her bag*
and gets out of the car.)
ERROL: What's the matter with you?
(YVETTE *slams the front passenger door.*)

EXT. OUTSIDE EFFRA HALL TAVERN. EVENING.
STUART *stands on the pavement and looks at* YVETTE.
STUART: What's the matter?
YVETTE: (*Snaps*) Nothing.
(YVETTE *begins to walk off down Kellett Road towards*
Atlantic Road. STUART *watches her, then he gets in the*
car. The car begins to pull away. YVETTE *stops. She looks*
up and follows it down the road. Then she continues to
walk.)

INT. BMW. EVENING.
ERROL *and* STUART *say nothing to each other. There is an*
uneasiness between them.

EXT. BRIXTON ROAD – OUTSIDE TOWN HALL, NEAR TO
FURNITURE SHOP. EVENING.
ERROL *pulls up for a traffic light.*

INT. BMW. EVENING.
STUART: You shouldn't be so hard on her.
ERROL: On who?
STUART: You know, Yvette.
ERROL: You her social worker?
STUART: No.
(ERROL *looks across at* STUART, *who looks away.*)

EXT. AT TRAFFIC LIGHTS, BRIXTON ROAD. EVENING.
The lights change and ERROL *drives on.*

INT. VILLAGE PUB. EVENING.
FREDRICK *stands at the bar talking with* JOHN, *the landlord. He is*

a stout man in his thirties. On the bar top is a collecting box for 'African Famine Relief'.

FREDRICK: I wouldn't rule out trouble.

JOHN: So you'll be having a word with the constable, then?

FREDRICK: Perhaps. There's drugs to contend with. It's part of their culture. And they're liable to burn a few buildings down if things don't go their way.

JOHN: Don't talk bloody wet, Fred.

FREDRICK: Talking wet, am I? Read a paper lately, have you? Watched any telly? It's all there for you to see, and whether you like it or not, facts are facts. There's no point in burying our heads in the sand.

EXT/INT.   VILLAGE CHEMIST.   EVENING.

SANDRA is preparing to close up for the night. She is in her early twenties. She looks both tired and bored. Her friend JULIE is watching her. She is slightly younger and a little more sprightly.

JULIE: Have you found out when Colin's next leave is?

SANDRA: When his sergeant says. Which might be never for all I know.

(*JULIE is trying some nail varnish.*)

SANDRA: What are you doing with that?

JULIE: Just looking.

SANDRA: Well, put it back: I'll get killed if anything's missing or broken.

JULIE: (*Puts it down*) What you doing tonight?

(*SANDRA locks the till. She is ready now.*)

SANDRA: Studio 54 with Warren. Then Breakfast at Tiffany's.

JULIE: Come on, Sand.

(*SANDRA begins to usher her towards the door. She changes the 'Open' sign to 'Closed'.*)

SANDRA: Watch my mother do her corns, then listen to her miscarriage stories. Wanna come round?

(*They pass through the door and SANDRA closes it behind them.*)

EXT.   VILLAGE SQUARE.   EVENING.

Across the square the slide show crowd are filing out of the village

hall, GODFREY, MARJORIE, VICAR, VIV *and* DEREK *and the*
COLONEL *are amongst the crowd. The three lads,* IAN, MICK *and*
SONNY *sit outside the village pub drinking pints.* SANDRA *and*
JULIE *come around the corner of the road at the side of the village*
hall.
SANDRA: (*Looking across at the hall*) The march of the bloody
    walking dead.
    (JULIE *looks at her.*)
IAN: (*Shouting across*) Fancy a pint, girls?
SANDRA: Yeah, we'll come back tomorrow when you've finished
    that one.

INT.   BRIXTON PUB.   NIGHT.
The pub is a shabby but friendly Brixton pub. The wall is painted
with Caribbean land- and seascapes. The juke box is loud. The
atmosphere is crowded and smoky. The conversation on this Friday
night is energetic.
Behind the bar there are two attractive black girls serving: one is tall,
the other slightly shorter.
About three quarters of the people in the pub are West Indian,
ranging from the age of twenty to sixty. Some are bearded, some look
tired from hard work, others look like they're on the dole. There are a
few Rastas among the crowd. A few West Indian women in their
forties, four or five white women – two middle-aged, two younger –
some are obviously hustlers. Some younger black guys fairly well
dressed, curly perm, others with short sides, long on top.
At a table in a back room next to the bar are ROBBO, *late forties,*
still wearing his London Transport uniform. He is the oldest friend of
WILLIE BOY *who is not yet there.*
LOUIS *is in his late thirties – still young enough to consider himself a*
bit dapper. Tall, good-looking, balding on the top. He wears drape
trousers, nice shirt, leather jacket. He sits with PAT *who is in her late*
twenties. She has locks, wears longish flowing skirt, loosish blouse,
belt, African-looking accessories, soft canvas shoes.
STEADROY *and* BOOTS *are also in their late twenties.* STEADROY
has on jeans, shirt, sneakers, and a tam. He listens to his Walkman.
BOOTS *is his shadow and friend and dresses similarly to* STEADROY.
He can't get a job so he 'hangs out'.

WILF *is in his forties. He runs a West Indian bakery. He wears a
well-worn but respectable suit. He sits with* DESERT HEAD. *He is
the same age as* WILF. *He is tall, completely bald and a little 'slow'.
He has on tight trousers, T-shirt.*
WILLIE BOY *comes in the pub and threads his way towards the
group. He is in his late forties. He has on worn-looking light
trousers, summer shirt and light jacket. Nothing looks new or in the
latest style.* WILLIE BOY *passes two uniformed policemen finishing a
conversation with one of the girls behind the bar. Then they walk out
of the pub but we don't hear what they are saying.* WILLIE BOY
continues walking through the pub.
WILLIE BOY: Everybody reach?
ROBBO: Neither Jeff nor Alfie make it as yet.

    (WILLIE BOY *takes out a team list and begins to look
    down it.*)

WILLIE BOY: (*To* ROBBO) What about Jeff now? He's coming or what?

ROBBO: How the frig you expect me to know? I nobody's keeper.

BOOTS: And nobody seen the two youths as yet.

WILLIE BOY: One of them nearly mash me down. I suppose the other one can't be far behind.

BOOTS: Well, we can still make a team meeting without them.

WILLIE BOY: Okay then. Since last week I been in touch with the people and, weather permitting, the game is on as planned.

STEADROY: Look, man, I have a blues to play at.

ROBBO: You didn't tell us nothing. Some of us maybe got other arrangements.

DESERT HEAD: I don't have nothing to do.

BOOTS: Except look for your brain.

WILF: No need to talk to him like that. Maybe you should look for a job instead of chatting rubbish.

WILLIE BOY: Okay, okay, listen everybody. Brixton Conquistadors versus Sneddington. 2 p.m. Sunday. Forty overs per innings. No bowler to bowl more than eight overs. Normal Sunday one-day rules. We must leave in the morning so we can make a weekend of it. (*To* LOUIS) You can get the coach to the Brixton Recreation Centre by nine?

LOUIS: No problem. But somebody should maybe get some directions. I never hear of a place name Sneddington.

STEADROY: And what we going do about accommodation tomorrow night?

WILLIE BOY: They agree to give us a place to stay, and entertain us as part of their African Famine week.

ROBBO: Listen, I know what these English people can be like, you know. I'm not staying in no fucking stable so let me make that crys-tal clear.

BOOTS: Your wife looks like an animal so you should be used to it.

ROBBO: (*Jumping up as if he's going to hit him*) You better watch your frigging mouth don't swallow your head, you hear? (*The others are holding* ROBBO *back.*)

9

LOUIS: (*Stands up*) Take it easy, Robbo. Just rest yourself, man. Everybody drinking the same again?
(*There are general murmurs of agreement 'Yes man', 'Sure', etc.*)
LOUIS: Pat?
PAT: Orange juice.

EXT.   BRIXTON STREET OUTSIDE ATLANTIC PUB.   NIGHT.
*A Renault Fuego pulls up outside the pub. Through the windscreen we can see a well-dressed man (*JEFF*) is driving. He is in his thirties. In the passenger seat is his wife, *ANGIE*. She is Jeff's age. She is English. In her arms she carries a baby. The car hazard warning lights come on.*
The car is parked temporarily.

INT/EXT.   FUEGO.   NIGHT.
*The engine is running. Indecision in the air. Then *JEFF* turns off the engine. Silence. He looks across at *ANGIE* who refuses to meet his eyes.*
ANGIE: Jeff?
JEFF: I won't be long.
(JEFF *gets out and shuts the door behind him. He walks around the front of the car. The two uniformed policemen who had been in the pub before walk past the pub.*
ANGIE *watches as he makes his way around the front of the car and disappears into the pub.*)

INT.   ATLANTIC PUB.   NIGHT.
JEFF *comes into the pub. He looks around for a moment, then he sees the others.* LOUIS *is just returning from the bar with the drinks.* JEFF *begins to pick his way across the pub towards them.*
BOOTS: William Whitelaw reach.
JEFF: Have I missed anything?
BOOTS: Sit down and take a drink. Take the weight off your suit.
(JEFF *sits. Looks at* PAT *who gives him a hard look and turns away.*)
LOUIS: (*Moves to get up – to* JEFF) You taking a Pils?

JEFF: No thanks. Not just yet.
(LOUIS *sits back down.*)
WILLIE BOY: (*To* JEFF) Well, it look like the team pick itself.
But Alfie still don't show as yet.
BOOTS: Or the youth.
JEFF: I see.
WILLIE BOY: We meeting at nine o'clock at the Recreation
Centre. (*To* PAT) Pat, you can sort out some food for the
journey?
PAT: I'll see what I can do.
WILLIE BOY: Wilf, you can bring some bread from your
bakery?
WILF: Sure, man.
(STEADROY *has been tampering with the sound system. It
accidentally crashes out at full volume.*)
LOUIS: Jesus, Steadroy, you trying to deaf us?
STEADROY: Pardon? (*He laughs at his own joke. Nobody else
does.*)
WILLIE BOY: Jeff, you coming on like a pussycat on a hot tin
roof. Just relax, man.
JEFF: (*Stands up*) I have the wife and child waiting for me.
WILLIE BOY: You can't bring them in?
JEFF: (*Giving* WILLIE BOY *a hard look*) I check you tomorrow,
okay?
(JEFF *moves back through the crowd and out of the door. Their
eyes follow him as he leaves.*)
BOOTS: I thought slavery done.

EXT/INT. VILLAGE PUB. NIGHT.
A drunk FREDRICK *leans against the bar and starts to try and get
people's attention. His audience is* MICK, IAN *and* SONNY,
SANDRA *and* JULIE, TOMMY *and* DAVID *and a few local
drinkers.*
FREDRICK: Ladies and gentlemen, your attention please. (*He
bangs his glass against the bartop.* JOHN *looks resigned.*) Just a
little turn to liven up the evening.
MICK: Cabaret, is it?
FREDRICK: You could say.

MICK: Well, carry on then, Miss Minnelli.

IAN: Oi! Where's your black stockings and suspender belt?

INT.   VILLAGE TAVERN.   NIGHT.

This is the upper middle class equivalent of the village pub. On the walls are old RAF memorabilia, hunting trophies, etc. The BARMAN *is a blazered and cravatted individual. On the bar top is a collecting box for 'African Famine Relief'.*
DEREK *and* KEVIN *stand by the bar.* KEVIN *is* DEREK's *best friend. The same age, the same Oxbridge mould. The* BARMAN *is just finishing serving* MISS RYE, *a retired spinster. There are some other elderly people in the pub.*

BARMAN: (*To* MISS RYE) There we are. A bottle of stout. Anything else?

MISS RYE: No, thank you.

(*They watch as she goes out.*)

KEVIN: I've never understood why she lives so far out. She's like an ex-nun cloistered away.

DEREK: You can't have an ex-nun. Once you're in you're in.

KEVIN: As the actress said to the bishop.

(DEREK *and* KEVIN *fall about laughing. The* BARMAN *rings a bell and calls 'Time!'*)

INT.   VILLAGE PUB.   NIGHT.

FREDRICK *is in full flow.*

FREDRICK: Why did the blind chicken cross the road?

MICK: To get away from you.

(*Everybody laughs at* FREDRICK, *who looks angrily at* MICK. *Then he prepares to tell another joke and everybody groans.*)

EXT.   OUTSIDE THE VILLAGE TAVERN.   NIGHT.

DEREK *and* KEVIN *emerge from the tavern into the street. They walk a few yards then* KEVIN *bowls an imaginary delivery.*

DEREK: 'Owzat!

(*They both laugh.*)

I've got it in.

KEVIN: Got what in?

DEREK: The box. I'm testing it out.

KEVIN: How's it feel?
DEREK: Good. Give it a whack.
    (KEVIN *gives* DEREK *a blow to the crotch.*)
DEREK: That's good. And again. This time harder.
    (*The village* CONSTABLE, *a middle-aged man with a beard,*
    sits astride his push-bike. The COLONEL, *tweed suit and*
    handlebar moustache, stands beside him. They look on unseen.)
COLONEL: Well, their preparation is thorough, if a trifle
    unorthodox.
    (*And* KEVIN *hits* DEREK *in the crotch. They both laugh and*
    start to walk on.)

INT. BEDROOM. NIGHT.
GODFREY *is lying in bed reading a book.*
MARJORIE *stares out ahead, her mind turning.*
MARJORIE: They'll be terribly good, won't they, Godfrey?
    (GODFREY *glances up.*)
    I expect they've been training for months.
GODFREY: Yes, I expect so.

INT. BASEMENT FLAT. NIGHT.
STEADROY *is holding a blues in this dark basement flat. The music*
crashes out of huge speakers. STEADROY *is the DJ. A few posters of*
black musicians on the walls (both reggae and soul). There is a side
room with a bar and food being sold. There are a couple of dozen people
listening to the dull bass rhythm, eating, smoking, leaning up against the
wall. The atmosphere is dark with a few coloured lights. Most of the
people are between nineteen and thirty with some on either side. There
are a few Rasta types, the rest are black soul kids, predominantly male.
YVETTE *and* MASIE *are the only two dancing in the small room*
where the speakers are. MASIE *is* YVETTE's *age. She is very like*
YVETTE *in appearance, i.e. no make-up. Plain in dress.*
The music continues and fills every inch of the basement flat.

INT/EXT. BMW. NIGHT.
ERROL *and* STUART *pull up outside a terraced house.* ERROL *turns*
off the engine. We hear the sound of music from the blues, which is
taking place in the basement of the house.

ERROL *looks in his rear-view mirror and lights a joint. He sees*
WILLIE BOY, BOOTS, ROBBO, LOUIS, WILF, DESERT HEAD *and*
PAT *pass them by.*
ERROL: Hang on a minute. Let Clive Lloyd lead the boys in.
> (*They cross in front of the car and go down into the basement of
> the house without noticing* ERROL *and* STUART.
> ERROL *passes the joint to* STUART *who takes a draw and starts
> to cough.* ERROL *looks at him, then sucks his teeth and snatches
> back the joint.*)

INT.   BASEMENT FLAT.   NIGHT.
WILLIE BOY *and his entourage come through the door and into the
blues. They greet people loudly and are obviously both welcome and
popular.*
LOUIS: Seem like we all need a drink?
FIRST MAN: (*Points to the kitchen*) Buy what you want through
> there.

INT.   BASEMENT FLAT.   NIGHT.
WILLIE BOY *comes through to where* YVETTE *and* MASIE *are. He
manages to talk to* YVETTE *above the music. She still dances.*
WILLIE BOY: Where the ruffians?
> (YVETTE *shrugs her shoulders.*)
> Well, you and Masie can help Pat out with the food
> tomorrow?
> (YVETTE *looks across at* MASIE *who nods.*)
YVETTE: What time?
WILLIE BOY: By nine at the Brixton Recreation Centre.
> (YVETTE *looks across at* MASIE *again who shrugs her shoulders
> and nods.* WILLIE BOY *looks as though he wants to say something
> else, but as* YVETTE *continues to dance he just stands instead.*)

INT.   BASEMENT FLAT.   NIGHT.
ERROL *and* STUART *come through the door. Before they can go
anywhere* ROBBO *holds* ERROL *by the sleeve.*
ROBBO: Where you been?
ERROL: I had business to take care of. (*Referring to his sleeve*)
> You want to buy my jacket?

(*People start to laugh at this.* ROBBO *sucks his teeth.* STUART *disappears into the room with food and drink.*)

BOOTS: (*Pointing to the joint*) Hey, youth, pass that thing there.

ERROL: Who you calling youth?

(ERROL *takes another draw and passes it over to* BOOTS. WILLIE BOY *comes through from the room with the sound system.*)

ROBBO: (*To* WILLIE BOY) Laurel and Hardy finally make it.

WILLIE BOY: What you mean by nearly running me over, boy?

ERROL: Is he talking to me?

WILLIE BOY: You little sharp-arse. You do that again and I throw down one set of blows on you.

(STUART *comes back out and gives* ERROL *a can of 'Red Stripe' beer.*)

ERROL: (*To* STUART) All right, man.

WILLIE BOY: You hear what I say?

ERROL: I'm not checking you, man, so why you don't just move?

(ERROL *goes to move past him but* WILLIE BOY *pushes him back.*)

WILLIE BOY: When I talking to you have some respect. And I want to know why you let my girl come in such a place on her own?

ERROL: Fuck off, man. I'm sick of you trying to big time everybody, fixing up games with white folk like you doing us a favour. Me, I don't want to play them people.

LOUIS: All right, I don't think we have any need for argument.

(*People are now beginning to stop what they are doing and watch.* YVETTE *and* MASIE *come out of the room with music to look and see what is going on.*)

WILLIE BOY: Argument what? I going cuff the little fucker.

(WILLIE BOY *grabs a bottle from the table,* STEADROY *grabs the arm holding the bottle.* WILF *tries to hold him back as* WILLIE BOY *looks like he is going to kill* ERROL. *The table falls over, drinks spill, bottles and glasses crash to the floor.* STEADROY *manages to grab the bottle from* WILLIE BOY's *hand.* ERROL *pushes by him and goes towards* YVETTE. *He puts his hand on her shoulder but she pushes him away and knocks him slightly off balance.*)

YVETTE: Don't touch me, Errol! I don't want to see you again.
  Understand!
  (YVETTE *pushes past everyone and moves to go out of the flat.*
  MASIE *makes like she is going to follow but* STUART *stops her.*)
STUART: No, I'll go. You wait here.
  (STUART *goes out of the door after* YVETTE.)

INT. BEDROOM. NIGHT.
VIV *stands over an ironing-board and finishes off Derek's white shirt.*
She unplugs the iron then hangs the shirt on a hanger with his cricket
flannels. She takes some care in how she arranges them.
DEREK *is propped up in bed alone. We see that he is reading the*
West Indian Cricket Annual. *He puts the book down and thinks*
for a moment. VIV *hangs his whites in the wardrobe.* DEREK *does*
not seem to have noticed.

EXT. ON THE BALCONY OF A RANGE OF FLATS. NIGHT.
We are on the tenth floor of an open range of council flats. From this
balcony we get an almost panoramic view of South London at night.
We see the lift arrive and WILLIE BOY *and* ROBBO *come out and*
walk towards us. ROBBO *seems a little unsure on his feet.*
WILLIE BOY: (*Stops outside his door and digs into his pocket for the*
  key) You have to sleep on the settee, you know.
ROBBO: If I go home that's where Celia going make me sleep
  anyhow.
  (WILLIE BOY *opens the door and they both go in. Hold as the*
  door slams shut.)

INT. FRONT ROOM OF WILLIE BOY'S FLAT. NIGHT.
The living room is clearly the scene of an on-going battle. YVETTE
tries to keep it clean; WILLIE BOY *leaves his newspaper, plates,*
shoes, etc. around.
ROBBO *is sprawled on the settee.* WILLIE BOY *sets a bottle of*
whisky and two glasses on the coffee table. He pulls up an armchair.
He begins to pour, and then passes ROBBO *the drink.*
WILLIE BOY: Seems like Yvette don't reach home as yet.
ROBBO: You not worried?
WILLIE BOY: She's twenty-one, man.

ROBBO: I wish I can act so cool.

WILLIE BOY: Well, you used to. I don't understand what happen to your head lately.

ROBBO: Celia beginning to cheese me off. I tell her I'm going home this Christmas for six weeks. Look a job. Explore the possibilities. You know what I mean.

WILLIE BOY: And what she say?

ROBBO: She say if I go, I mustn't bother to come back. She say we'll go together or none of us. (*Pause.*) But I going, man.

WILLIE BOY: Why you don't send her?

ROBBO: So she stay over there like Mildred done you.

WILLIE BOY: (*Snaps*) Mildred supposed to stay, so what you trying to say?

ROBBO: Nothing, man, but I thought you suppose to follow.

WILLIE BOY: I will. You think I making joke?

(ROBBO *takes a big gulp of whisky.*)

ROBBO: But when, man! When! Don't you see that's just it. I was twenty-three when I make the biggest decision of my life as to whether to cross the Atlantic and put a whole new perspective on my future. Now look at me, man. Nearly fifty and I fucking up myself trying to make the same decision again; the same frigging thing in reverse.

WILLIE BOY: Take it easy, Robbo. Take it easy, man.

ROBBO: (*Kicking off his shoes*) Look man, knock off the light. Let me catch a sleep here before morning come. My head killing me and I don't want to run off my mouth in your face.

WILLIE BOY: (*Standing*) You know where everything is?

ROBBO: Yes, man, yes.

(*Pause, they look at each other.*)

Look, man, I better sleep otherwise I going drive the two of us crazy with question and no answer. I check you in the morning.

WILLIE BOY: Later, man, later. Sleep good. And stop your worrying.

(WILLIE BOY *snaps off the light but goes nowhere. He looks as* ROBBO *stretches out full length, then turns over on the settee.*

WILLIE BOY *walks over to the window and looks out over*
South London and then draws the curtains.
ROBBO *is restless; he is going to have a bad night's sleep.*)

EXT.   SNEDDINGTON VILLAGE GREEN.   MORNING.
An early morning wide shot establishes that we are back in
Sneddington. It is a fresh and clear morning. All seems tranquil,
apart from a group of villagers trying to erect a marquee on the edge
of the green and to the side of a neat and whitewashed pavilion.
DEREK *and* KEVIN *are the brains behind the operation.* VIV *is trying*
to lend a hand. MARJORIE *looks on.*
VIV: Push a little more on your side, Kevin.
DEREK: (*Racing around pushing pegs into the ground*) Okay, I've
   got it.
   (DEREK *and* KEVIN *step back and it stays up.*)
MARJORIE: It looks so pretty. Like a sail on a ship fluttering
   away. It's a shame we can't have it here all the time.
   (*The three of them look at her like she's slightly mad.* KEVIN
   takes out a handkerchief and begins to mop his brow.)
KEVIN: I'm jiggered.
MARJORIE: I'm sure Godfrey would have come but he's terribly
   busy this morning.

INT.   ROSE COTTAGE.   MORNING.
GODFREY *is playing snooker. He is in a wood shed at the back of*
the garden which is painted black inside and out with a couple of
windows. The room is in semi-darkness other than the morning light
breaking through the window and the light from the low hanging
billiards light over the table. By the side of the table sits his dog.
GODFREY *clears blue, pink, then black, concentrating hard with*
each shot. As soon as he has potted the black he starts to rack up
again for another frame against himself. He talks to the dog.
GODFREY: That's what's known as a clean-up. Blue, pink,
   black. A crucial trio. Often the match-winning break.
   Practice. Attention to detail.

EXT.   BRIXTON RECREATION CENTRE.   MORNING.
The small coach on which the team will be travelling is parked

*outside the Recreation Centre. It is an old coach but it looks solid
enough. It has been borrowed or rented from a West Indian company
and this is evident from the sign on the side of the coach.*

LOUIS *and* WILLIE BOY *stand on top of the stairs waiting. We see
the rest of the team on the coach.*

WILLIE BOY: How many to come?

LOUIS: Three or four still. (*Looks at his watch*) It's quarter past
    nine. Why these people can't keep any time?

WILLIE BOY: Maybe we should take a team photo while we
    wait. (*He produces a Kodak disc camera.*)

LOUIS: A what?

WILLIE BOY: A team photo. For a souvenir. And for the
    records. (*He walks downstairs towards the coach.*)

LOUIS: What records?

INT/EXT. ON COACH. MORNING.

WILLIE BOY *puts his head around the corner of the door and shouts down the aisle. People are still trying to settle in for the journey.*

WILLIE BOY: We going take a team photo so everyone off the coach.

WILF: Alfie still don't show.

WILLIE BOY: Well then, he miss the picture. (*Pause.*) And anyway what happen? You married to Alfie?
(*There is a general moaning as everyone starts to get up and file back down the aisle and off the coach again.*)

EXT. RECREATION CENTRE. MORNING.

As they pile off the coach WILLIE BOY *busily arranges everyone into a group formation on the stairs. As he does so* YVETTE *and* STUART *walk up the road towards the others.*

WILLIE BOY: (*To* YVETTE) You all right? I couldn't find you this morning.

YVETTE: I wasn't there. I only went home about half an hour ago.

WILLIE BOY: Where were you?

YVETTE: Just out. I'll explain later.

WILLIE BOY: Out where?

YVETTE: (*Looks at her father slightly embarrassed that he is quizzing her in front of everybody.*) I'll explain later, Dad. (YVETTE *walks off and goes upstairs to join* MASIE *for the group photograph.* WILLIE BOY *re-composes himself. Like everyone else,* STUART *has been watching what has just happened. He goes across to* ERROL *to join him for the photograph.*)

STUART: How you doing, man?

(ERROL *sucks his teeth and ignores him.* WILLIE BOY *squats on one knee with his Kodak disc camera.*)

WILLIE BOY: You look like a chain gang. The least some of you can do is uncurl your top lip.

BOOTS: Hurry up, man. We don't have all day.

STEADROY: (*Squatting down*) Boy, my back beginning to hurt me, you know.

WILLIE BOY: Nearly ready. Wilf, move in.

WILF: (*Standing at the side*) In where?

WILLIE BOY: Into the picture, you fool (WILF *does so.*) Okay, hold it. Smile.

(WILLIE BOY *takes the photograph. Then those who are sitting stand up and everyone walks down the stairs and begins to move back towards the coach.*)

I better take a safety shot just to make sure.

BOOTS: In that case you better find somebody else to take it of. We finish.

WILLIE BOY: What the hell kind of team spirit is this?

(*A silverish Renault Fuego turns into the Brixton Recreation Centre and parks. We see a hurried-looking* JEFF *get out of the passenger side and go around to the boot. He takes out a kit bag, then a briefcase and shuts the boot.* JEFF *moves around to the driver's side to kiss* ANGIE *'Goodbye', but she turns the car around and drives off.*)

JEFF *turns around and looks across to where* WILLIE BOY *is standing.*)
WILLIE BOY: (*Shouts*) We don't have all day, Jeff.
(JEFF *walks towards* WILLIE BOY.)
(*Indicating the direction from which the car has left*) Anything I can do to help?
JEFF: You know anybody in the Mafia?
WILLIE BOY: It reach that stage?
(JEFF *gets on the coach.* WILLIE BOY *moves to follow.*)

EXT. BRIXTON RECREATION CENTRE. MORNING.
The coach pulls out of the Recreation Centre. It stops at the edge of the road and waits before someone flashes it through and into the traffic.

EXT. MOTORWAY. MORNING.
We see the coach on a spaghetti-type junction leading out to the motorway. It tears past us and up the motorway. It passes signs to Suffolk.

EXT. VILLAGE SQUARE. MORNING.
SONNY, MICK *and* IAN *are standing outside the pub waiting for it to open. Behind them we can see* MARJORIE *trying to organize a brass band in the square under the war memorial. She is trying to do one thing, and the* COLONEL, *who is the leader of the brass band, is trying to do another.* KEVIN, DEREK *and* VIV *walk across the square and join the three lads.*
DEREK: Not open yet, then?
IAN: We wouldn't be stood here if he was.
DEREK: Good, I can see we're on the ball today.
MICK: You lot put that tent up?
KEVIN: We have, no thanks to you I might add.
MICK: It's your problem. We're not labourers.
DEREK: (*Aside to* VIV) Shouldn't you be getting back now?
VIV: What for? They'll be here soon.
DEREK: I thought we might have a spot of lunch first. Kevin and I will just have a quick one then we'll be along.
VIV: (*Agitated, she whispers now*) Well, I'd quite like a drink myself, Derek.

22

(*We hear* JOHN *opening the door to the pub. Then he stands before them.*)
JOHN: Anyone would think I was giving the ale away free.
DEREK: (*To* VIV) I'll see you in a short while then.
   (VIV *does not reply. She simply stares at* DEREK *annoyed and upset. Then she turns and walks away.*
   Hold on DEREK'*s face as he looks at her walking off.*)

INT/EXT.   ON COACH.   AFTERNOON.
The coach is speeding along the motorway.
LOUIS *has put on a soft soul music cassette.* ERROL *and* STUART *sit together.*
ERROL: How you mean she stayed by you last night?
STUART: I told you, we both sat and talked.
ERROL: You fuck her?
STUART: Don't be a prick.
ERROL: You think there's something wrong with me asking?
STUART: No. (*Pause.*) Have you finished with her then?
   (ERROL *just looks at him.*)

EXT.   MOTORWAY.   AFTERNOON.
From a bridge we have a shot of the coach speeding along the motorway towards us. It passes under the bridge.

INT/EXT.   ON COACH.   AFTERNOON.
Later. The music is now lover's rock. WILLIE BOY *and* ROBBO *are at the front of the coach bent double over a map. Eventually* WILLIE BOY *looks up at* LOUIS.
WILLIE BOY: You know where we are?
LOUIS: You supposed to be the navigator.
WILLIE BOY: In that case we lost.
   (LOUIS *looks at him as if to say 'Can't you read a map?' He flicks on the indicator and begins to take a slip road.*)

EXT.   PETROL STATION.   AFTERNOON.
At the foot of the slip road there is a petrol station. We have the POV of the PETROL PUMP ATTENDANT, *who is a man of about thirty. He looks up and sees the coach pulling in. The doors open and*

the music comes out to meet him. Then WILLIE BOY, ROBBO *and* LOUIS *get out.* BOOTS *and* DESERT HEAD *get out behind them.*

BOOTS: Where the toilets?

(*The* PETROL PUMP ATTENDANT *points.* BOOTS *and* DESERT HEAD *go off.*)

LOUIS: Can you tell us the quickest way to Suffolk?

PETROL PUMP ATTENDANT: Probably fly.

(*This is the first time they have come across an East Anglian accent.* ROBBO, LOUIS *and* WILLIE BOY *look at each other, not sure if he's taking the piss.*)

PETROL PUMP ATTENDANT: You want to go back the way you've just come. When you see the signs for Cambridge turn off to your left. Where is it exactly you want to be?

WILLIE BOY: Sneddington.

PETROL PUMP ATTENDANT: Never heard of it. But you should be all right if you go in that direction. And I see you've got a map.

LOUIS: (*Sarcastic*) I know. That's why we're here.

(*The* PETROL PUMP ATTENDANT *walks away and goes into his booth. We see* BOOTS *and* DESERT HEAD *coming back from the toilet.* WILLIE BOY, LOUIS, ROBBO *turn and join them. They get on the coach and* LOUIS *starts up the engine.*)

EXT. MOTORWAY. AFTERNOON.
The coach is hurtling along in the opposite direction now. We watch it pass under the bridge going back where it has just come from.

INT/EXT. ON COACH. AFTERNOON.
WILLIE BOY *and* ROBBO *still look anxiously at the map.*

WILLIE BOY: (*Scratches his head*) You know, I sure we still going the wrong way.

(*They drive on for a short while. Then they see an English family picnicking on the hard shoulder of the motorway.*)

ROBBO: You think we should stop for some food?

(WILLIE BOY *shrugs his shoulders.*)

EXT. HARD SHOULDER OF THE MOTORWAY. AFTERNOON.
PAT *is perched on a fence drinking a tumbler of ginger beer and*

eating a sandwich. A clumsy JEFF *is holding a patty and struggling to join her on the fence. He slips and steps in some cowshit.*

JEFF: Bloody hell!

PAT: (*Sarcastically*) Not to worry, I'm sure there's somebody who'll clean it off for you.

EXT.   HARD SHOULDER OF THE MOTORWAY.   AFTERNOON.
WILLIE BOY *holds a sandwich and the map. He is trying to talk to* LOUIS *with his mouth full.* BOOTS *looks on.*

WILLIE BOY: (*Gestures to the map again and then to the motorway*) I'm telling you, man. In this book this road don't exist.

BOOTS: You are both real dumbos. I am going to ask somebody. (BOOTS *wanders off into the inside lane of the motorway and tries to flag down a speeding car. It swerves and sounds its horn.*)

WILLIE BOY: (*He drops the map and his sandwich*) Jesus Christ!

25

(*He rushes into the motorway and grabs* BOOTS.)
What the fuck you doing?
BOOTS: I'm trying to help, man. We could be here all day.

INT/EXT.   ON COACH.   AFTERNOON.
They are speeding along the motorway. ROBBO *has taken over the map-reading and squats next to* LOUIS. WILLIE BOY *sits and looks at them. He seems fed up.* PAT, MASIE *and* YVETTE *are handing around the food.* YVETTE *stands holding a Tupperware bowl full of chicken legs in front of* ERROL. PAT *pushes her on down the aisle.*
PAT: Girl, if he don't want to take one then leave him.

INT.   KITCHEN.   AFTERNOON.
VIV *has on an apron. She is clearing up the table. It is clear two people have just eaten. She scrapes some food into the dustbin. Then runs the taps to wash up. The clock in the hallway chimes. She looks up at the kitchen clock and sees it is quarter to two. She pulls out the plug from the kitchen sink and tears off her apron.*

INT/EXT.   ON COACH.   AFTERNOON.
The coach still speeds along the motorway. A reggae tape is playing now. LOUIS *points at the map and smiles.* ROBBO *stands up and turns to the rest of the coach.*
ROBBO: Okay, we soon reach. We have everything figured out now.
   (*Happy, though slightly cynical, applause from everybody.*)
STEADROY: (*To* LOUIS) Turn it up, man. It's a hard tune.
   (LOUIS *turns up the music.* STEADROY *starts to sing.* BOOTS *joins him for the chorus. And soon the whole coach is singing.*)

EXT.   MOTORWAY SLIP ROAD.   AFTERNOON.
We see the coach coming towards us. Its indicators show it is about to take the slip road. It passes by and out of frame.

EXT.   LEAFY COUNTRY LANE.   AFTERNOON.
Later. Medium shot of the coach as it takes a tight bend in a country lane.

26

EXT. BY PARISH CHURCH. AFTERNOON.

*We are looking down a peaceful country lane with medieval houses
on either side. At the end of the lane is a magnificent parish church.
From around the corner the coach comes into view.*

We see GODFREY, *meandering along. He has on a tweed jacket, hat
and carries a walking stick. By his side is the dog. He looks up and
sees the coach coming towards him. He stands and watches as it
passes him by.*

EXT. VILLAGE SQUARE. AFTERNOON.

FREDRICK *is sitting outside the pub with his two teenage sons,*
TOMMY *and* DAVID. *Sitting with them are* SONNY, IAN, MICK
and SANDRA *and* JULIE. *They chat and drink in the afternoon sun.
The local brass band continue to tune up. Standing by the band, and
obviously forming some sort of reception committee are* MARJORIE
(with clipboard), MISS RYE, DEREK, KEVIN *and* VIV. *The* VICAR
stands with them.

Cut to shot of the village CONSTABLE *perched on his bike at a diplomatic distance between the pub group and the reception committee group.*
In the distance we hear the coach. Then the COLONEL *appears over the brow of the hill and makes a signal for the band to get ready.*
COLONEL: They're here!
　　(*No sooner is the message received than the band strikes up, and the coach begins to appear over the hill. As it comes fully into view we realize the small brass band are playing 'Island In The Sun'.*)

INT/EXT.　　ON COACH.　　AFTERNOON.
The team looks out of the window at their reception. LOUIS *begins to draw the coach to a halt.*
ROBBO: Jesus Christ, I hope they expecting somebody else.
BOOTS: Hey, Jeff, you going feel at home here.

(*They all laugh.*)

WILLIE BOY: (*Pointing to* BOOTS's *joint*) Look man, you want us
all banged up in jail?

BOOTS: You don't think England's a prison?

EXT. BY THE PARISH CHURCH. AFTERNOON.
GODFREY *is now in the fields behind the church. He stands and
listens to the strains of the brass band drifting down from the village
square. He listens for a few moments then snaps out of it. He bends
down and pats his dog. They walk off together.* GODFREY *throws a
piece of stick for the dog to chase.*

EXT. VILLAGE SQUARE. AFTERNOON.
*All of the West Indians have now got off the coach. They stand and
look around at the smiling faces. It is a bright day. Some shield their
eyes.*
MARJORIE *begins her speech without the aid of a PA system. She
shouts.*

MARJORIE: Today it's my great pleasure to welcome to Sneddington the successful West Indian cricket team from
Brixton, London. The Conquistadors.
(*Applause.*)
Their presence is a fitting climax to our Third World Week
and I'm sure I speak for all of Sneddington in hoping that
the weekend is a happy and successful one.
(WILLIE BOY *is ushered forward. Clearly he is expected to
make a speech.*)

WILLIE BOY: Thank you, thank you. Well, we pleased to be
here. All of us. And naturally we hoping to give you a good
game. (*He digs into his holdall and pulls out a Tesco bag.
From inside he takes out an embroidered pennant with a
Jamaican flag on it.*)
Most of the boys is Jamaican so it's a majority decision.

BOOTS: (*Under his breath, but audible*) I ain't no fucking
Jamaican.
(WILLIE BOY *gives him a sharp look.*)

WILLIE BOY: We had a whip round. We'd like to give you this.
(*More applause.* KEVIN *produces a very flash camera. He*

29

'snaps' WILLIE BOY 'presenting' the pennant to MARJORIE.)

MARJORIE: Now in a couple of hours the Vicar will be having a small reception. Until then we had better get you all billeted. Derek and Vivien are able to take up to four. If there are any volunteers?

(*The West Indians just look at each other. Nobody makes a move.* MISS RYE *puts her hand up for* MARJORIE *to see. She then walks over to* WILLIE BOY.)

MISS RYE: I am Miss Rye, and you?

WILLIE BOY: Willie Boy.

MISS RYE: Pleased to meet you. (*She shakes his hand.*) Well, Mister Willie Boy, you will be staying with me.

(*Without waiting for him to answer, she hums and starts to walk away.* WILLIE BOY *is forced to follow her.*)

EXT.   COUNTRY LANE.   AFTERNOON.

WILLIE BOY *is riding an old push bike. He is following* MISS RYE. *She pedals ahead.*

MISS RYE: (*Pointing unnecessarily to the church*) There, Mister Willie Boy, is our church.

(*She takes a right hand turn at the side of the church.* WILLIE BOY *is clearly struggling, out of breath and lagging.*)

MISS RYE: Not far now. Only a mile or so.

(*We track them for a short while then let them pass into the distance.*)

EXT.   THE ROSE GARDEN.   AFTERNOON.

ERROL *and* STUART *are sitting outside in what is a classic English country garden. Behind them is a thatched cottage.*

MARJORIE *puts down a tray on which there is a jug of lemonade and a plate of cakes.*

MARJORIE: Just give me a shout if you need anything else.

ERROL/STUART: Thanks.

(MARJORIE *leaves.* ERROL *puts his hand into the jug of lemonade and brings out a pip that he flicks to one side.*)

ERROL: Slackness, man. Slackness.

(GODFREY *and the dog come through the gate and walk towards them.*)

GODFREY: Afternoon.

ERROL: (*Gesturing to the drink*) You have any ice?

GODFREY: (*Thinks*) Ice? We never had any ice. Black people were cool enough.

(GODFREY *chuckles to himself and passes out of sight the way* MARJORIE *went.*)

STUART: Who's he?

ERROL: The butler, man. All these people have servants and thing.

(*They both start to laugh.*)

EXT. DEREK AND VIV'S HOUSE. AFTERNOON.

INT. KITCHEN. AFTERNOON.

JEFF, PAT, LOUIS *and* BOOTS *are sat at the kitchen table.* VIV *is chopping onions, radishes, etc. to make a salad.* DEREK *is putting linseed oil on to his bat. There are newspapers, etc. spread on the floor.*

DEREK: (*To* BOOTS) You bowl what, then? Finger spin, the swinging off-break, fast yorkers?

BOOTS: Strictly pace.

DEREK: Killing the game though, isn't it.

(*He reaches for the* West Indian Cricket Annual *and gives it to* BOOTS.)

Just glance through that and you'll find Ramadhin, Valentine, Gibbs. Great spinners. I don't understand why all of a sudden you chaps want to be speed merchants.

VIV: (*Gesturing to the book*) Derek's been doing his homework.

DEREK: Well, after all that's a captain's job.

LOUIS: So you feel you can take us then?

DEREK: (*Demonstrates a leg glance with his bat*) I'm quietly confident.

BOOTS: (*Tosses down the* Annual) You want to make a raas clart bet then?

(PAT *kicks* BOOTS *under the table.* DEREK *laughs uneasily.*)

DEREK: (*Puts down his bat, to* JEFF) So what do you do?

JEFF: I work in race relations.

DEREK: Not much call for that around here.

EXT.   VICAR'S LAWN.   AFTERNOON.

The lawn behind the vicarage. The whole scene is bathed in sunshine. There is a party for about forty people, 'the pillars of society'. A string quartet plays. The West Indians mix.

WOMAN'S VOICE: Ronald, I'd like you to meet Boots, is it?

MAN'S VOICE: That's a rather agricultural name, isn't it?

(ERROL *stands to one side with a* WAITER.)

ERROL: You can't see that they're oppressing you?

WAITER: Oppressing us?

EXT.   COUNTRY LANE.   AFTERNOON.

We are on the outskirts of the village. WILLIE BOY *and* MISS RYE *are cycling back now. They're riding down a country road just before you come to a stream with a pink house by it. They are dressed in different outfits from earlier. They pass a couple of villagers out walking.*

VILLAGERS: Afternoon!

MISS RYE: Afternoon!

(WILLIE BOY *is struggling badly.*)

WILLIE BOY: (*Shouts*) I can't make it!

(*He brakes and falls off the bike on to a grassy verge.* MISS RYE *cycles back to him.*)

MISS RYE: Mr Willie Boy? Are you all right?

WILLIE BOY: Jesus Christ, I can't feel my legs!

MISS RYE: Hurry up or we'll miss the vicar's tea party.

EXT. VICAR'S LAWN. AFTERNOON.
Later. The string quartet plays on.

ROBBO: (*To* LOUIS) Where the hell is he?

LOUIS: I look like a clairvoyant to you? (*Pause.*) Look, man, let's just go. This thing almost finish anyhow.

INT. VILLAGE TAVERN. EVENING.
DEREK *is holding two silver trophies.* KEVIN *is trying to position him so that he can take a picture.*
The tavern is nearly empty.

KEVIN: Just a little to the side so the shaft of light catches you.

DEREK: Arty, eh. A real-life Snowdon, aren't we.

BARMAN: Don't you think it should be a team photograph?

DEREK: Do you want all those oiks in here?

EXT. VILLAGE SQUARE. EVENING.
Outside the pub sit ROBBO, LOUIS, JEFF, WILF, DESERT HEAD, PAT, YVETTE *and* MASIE. *They are talking with* FREDRICK, TOMMY, DAVID *and the three lads,* SONNY, MICK *and* IAN. STEADROY *and* BOOTS *are standing in the archway next to the pub.* BOOTS *is rolling a joint.*

STEADROY: You need more herbs?

(BOOTS *nods.*)

33

EXT. VILLAGE SQUARE. EVENING.

MISS RYE *cycles into the square. She looks fresh and breezy. She stops. She sits astride her bike and waits.*
A few moments later an exhausted WILLIE BOY *appears, pushing his bike. He leans it up against the village hall.*

MISS RYE: (*Looks over to the pub*) Well, your friends seem to have settled in all right. (*She turns to leave.*) I'll see you later then. Bye!

(WILLIE BOY *watches as she rides off down the hill. Then he walks slowly, and painfully, over to the war memorial and sits on his own.*)

INT. BACK ROOM OF THE PUB. EVENING.

It is gloomy. The sort of back room that's used only for pool.
STUART *is standing by the bar paying* JOHN *for two pints and two shorts.* SANDRA *and* JULIE *stand holding the cues.* ERROL *searches for the coins to put into the pool table.*

JOHN: (*Giving* STUART *his change*) I don't know. Pool on a nice evening like this.

SANDRA: It's either pool in here, or their conversation out there.

JOHN: If you need anything else just shout.

(*He leaves.* STUART *brings the drinks over.*)

SANDRA: So what's your names then?

ERROL: I'm Errol, he's Stuart.

SANDRA: Errol and Stuart. I'm Sandra and this . . .

JULIE: I *can* talk you know. I'm Julie.

SANDRA: All right!

(ERROL *puts the first thirty pence in the machine and the balls come out.*)

SANDRA: Shall I play with Errol to start with? Then we can swap round.

JULIE: I don't care. Whatever you like. (*To* STUART) Who do you want to play with?

STUART: You, I suppose.

JULIE: Well, that's settled then, isn't it.

(SANDRA *looks at her as if to say 'What's the matter with you, then?'*)

34

EXT.   UNDER WAR MEMORIAL IN VILLAGE SQUARE.
EVENING.

WILLIE BOY *sits alone under the war memorial. He looks up and sees* GODFREY *and the dog coming towards him. The sun begins to set.*

GODFREY: May we join you? (*He doesn't wait for an answer, just sits. Indicating the dog*) This is Polly. I'm Godfrey Matthews. Who are you?

WILLIE BOY: Willie Boy.

GODFREY: Nickname, is it?

WILLIE BOY: No. (*Pause.*) You lived here long?

(GODFREY *looks up at the scene outside the pub and laughs. Without turning to look at* WILLIE BOY *he answers.*)

GODFREY: My dear fellow, too long. (*Pause.*) Five years. Or six. I've lost count. Each day seems much like the next. (*Pause.*) Were those your sons I saw earlier in the day?

WILLIE BOY: Sons?

GODFREY: Tall boys. Striking – muscular.

WILLIE BOY: I have a daughter here with me. But no son.

GODFREY: I was going to ask them about games. About whether black men should play games in times such as these. If there aren't more serious considerations.

WILLIE BOY: Sure we should play games. Everybody has to relax. You only questioning it because black men always licking you.

GODFREY: That might be so. (*Pause.*) I once paid a brief visit to the Caribbean. Palm trees. Coconut trees. White beaches. Rum. Corrugated iron roofs. Poverty. Then I went back to Africa.

WILLIE BOY: You used to live in Africa?

GODFREY: For many years.

WILLIE BOY: You didn't like the Caribbean?

GODFREY: I loved it.

WILLIE BOY: What about the poverty?

GODFREY: I don't know. But don't be ashamed of poverty.

WILLIE BOY: I'm not ashamed. (*Pause.*) I'm going back.

GODFREY: (*Laughs*) You're going back. We're all going back.

WILLIE BOY: But it's where I'm from. I'm going back.

(GODFREY *says nothing.* WILLIE BOY *looks at him then stares out into the distance at the pub.*)

INT. BACK ROOM OF THE PUB. EVENING.
They are still playing doubles. ERROL *is at the table. He pots a good shot and* SANDRA *grabs his arm to congratulate him.*
SANDRA: That was great!
 (*He frees himself then plays a safety shot.*)
STUART: You're just lucky.
ERROL: The appliance of science. Play the game, man!
 (*The girls laugh.* STUART *looks across and notices* YVETTE *standing by the door.*)
STUART: I didn't see you standing there. Do you want a game?
 (YVETTE's *presence has changed the atmosphere.*)
JULIE: Come on, Stuart, aren't you playing?
YVETTE: I'm going for a walk.
 (*She turns and walks off.* STUART *hovers as if unable to decide what to do.*)
ERROL: (*Firmly*) It's your shot, man.
 (STUART *goes back to the table and the game goes on.*)

EXT. OUTSIDE PUB. EVENING.
YVETTE *comes out and passes* MASIE. PAT *and* LOUIS *are no longer there.* FREDRICK *is boring everyone to tears.*
FREDRICK: Well, it's one thing saying 'coloured', but it's quite a different thing saying 'black'. I mean for a start off there's different implications. Like on my farm. Black horses and white horses. The same, but different.
MASIE: (*She stands*) Where you going?
YVETTE: For a walk.
MASIE: Can I come?
YVETTE: On my own.
 (*A disappointed* MASIE *sits down.*)
MICK: (*To* YVETTE *as she leaves*) Can't we come?
IAN: Speak for yourself.
 (*The lads laugh.* YVETTE *walks off.* WILLIE BOY *does not see her although she sees him.*)
JEFF: (*Gets up*) I think I better be getting back now.

MASIE: I'll come with you.

FREDRICK: (*Leads the protests*) I was just going to buy you all another round. The night's still young.

ROBBO: You're going on like a fifteen-year-old, Jeff. Your wife not with you tonight, man.
  (JEFF *laughs nervously. Then he leaves.* MASIE *scuttles after him.*)

EXT.   UNDER WAR MEMORIAL IN VILLAGE SQUARE.
EVENING.

WILLIE BOY *looks across at the group outside the pub. He sees* JEFF *and* MASIE *walk off.*

GODFREY *stands and calls 'Polly'.*

GODFREY: Goodnight, Willie Boy. Sleep tight.

WILLIE BOY: Goodnight, man. I see you sometime tomorrow.
  (GODFREY *smiles at* WILLIE BOY *as he moves off in the opposite direction to* JEFF *and* MASIE. WILLIE BOY *watches him pass out of sight. Then he closes his eyes.*)

INT.   VILLAGE TAVERN.   NIGHT.

The tavern is quite full and lively. DEREK *and* KEVIN *sit together before a table full of empties.*

DEREK: So I said to him, 'What do you bowl then? Finger spin, off-break, yorkers?' And he said, 'Strictly pace.'
  (*He falls about laughing.*)

KEVIN: I don't get it. What does it mean?

DEREK: Strictly pace?

KEVIN: Yes. Does it mean fast?

DEREK: Well, that's what I thought he meant. (*Takes a drink*) I suppose we'll just have to wait until tomorrow to find out.

KEVIN: I'm not sure I want to find out.

INT.   KITCHEN.   NIGHT.

JEFF *is sitting at the table drinking a cup of coffee.* VIV *has on a dressing gown. She is smoking a cigarette as if unused to it.*

VIV: Pat went to bed hours ago. The other man, Louis, he's just gone up.

JEFF: I'll have to be quiet then.

38

VIV: (*Comes and sits at the table*) I'm sure he won't hear you. (*Pause.*) Is he your star player?

JEFF: Not really.

VIV: Oh you are!

JEFF: (*Laughs*) No, we don't really have one . . . Sometimes we don't even have a team . . . People only turn out when they think there's something in it for them. Like this, a weekend away from London.

VIV: I see. (*Pause.*) What time is your friend Boots coming back?

JEFF: I don't know. Is that a problem?

VIV: No, I'll just leave the back door open. He can let himself in. Derek always says it's one of the big advantages of living in the country. You don't have that security problem.

JEFF: I wouldn't know. I've always lived in the town.

VIV: I see. More coffee?
(*She gets up without waiting for an answer.*)

EXT. COUNTRY LANE. NIGHT.

YVETTE *is walking slowly along a country lane. She is not exactly sure of where she is. A car passes by and she stops at the side of the road. She freezes until it is out of sight. The night eventually extinguishes its red tail lights. Then she starts to walk on and another car passes her by. It stops some way past her then starts to reverse.* YVETTE *stands frightened. As it draws level with her she sees it is the three lads from the pub.* MICK *is driving.* SONNY *is next to him.* IAN *is in the back.* SONNY *rolls down his window.*

MICK: Are you lost?

YVETTE: A bit.

IAN: You're about two miles from the village. Do you want a lift back?

YVETTE: No, I'll walk if you just tell me which way.

MICK: You've got to be joking. All sorts of stuff happens to people out in these lanes. Come on, we'll drop you back.
(IAN *opens the back door.*)
Well?
(*After what seems like a cavernous pause* YVETTE *finally relents*

39

and gets in. The door slams and we follow the car as it pulls away.)

INT. KITCHEN. NIGHT.
VIV *is pouring herself a new cup of coffee.*
VIV: I hope you don't mind my asking, but are Pat and Louis together, because I put them in separate rooms?
JEFF: No. I don't think they're together.
VIV: She told me she had a four-year-old son. (*Pause.*) Is he the father of her child?
JEFF: No.
VIV: (*She comes to sit again*) I didn't mean to pry.
JEFF: I am. (*Pause.*) I'm the father.
VIV: It's all right. (*She puts out her cigarette.*) I won't tell anybody. (*Pause.*) You're married, aren't you?
JEFF: Nearly two years. I have a son of my own. Do you have any children?
VIV: We can't. Or at least we don't think we can. Derek's having tests.

40

JEFF: I'm sorry.

VIV: Don't be sorry. A baby would only complicate things.

JEFF: But do you want a child?

VIV: More than anything in the world.

(*They both hear someone coming down the stairs. The door opens and* PAT *stands before them in her dressing gown. She looks at them both.*)

PAT: I'm sorry. I only wanted a drink of water. (*She turns and walks out of the kitchen.* JEFF *won't look at* VIV.)

VIV: I'm sorry if I've caused you any trouble.

JEFF: No. (*Pause.*) It's nothing. You haven't caused any trouble.

(VIV *lights another cigarette.* JEFF *looks up.*)

VIV: Another coffee?

JEFF: No thanks. (*Pause.*) Don't you care for him?

VIV: (*Laughs*) Have you ever watched a candle go out?

JEFF: (*Touches her hand*) I can't understand why you're on your own. You're beautiful, you know.

(VIV *smiles.* JEFF *lowers his eyes.*)

41

Wrong time, though. Wrong place.
(VIV *leans over and kisses him.* JEFF *does not raise his eyes.*)

INT/EXT. IN CAR. NIGHT.
The three lads have driven the car to an abandoned, deserted farm.
MICK *and* SONNY *are screwed around in their seats so they are*
facing YVETTE. *She stares back defiantly.*
IAN: Well, what do you think we should do to you?
MICK: Could do anything really, couldn't we? Nobody would
    hear.
    (YVETTE *makes a grab at the door but* IAN *holds her.*)
IAN: You wouldn't get far. There's no one around for miles.
YVETTE: (*Quietly*) I'll kill you.
MICK: (*Mocking*) You'll do what?
YVETTE: I'll kill you.
    (*There is a long pause in which the lads don't know whether to*
    take her seriously or not.)
MICK: Okay, who's the first to be killed?
    (*They laugh nervously.*)
SONNY: Oh, come on. This is no good. Let's go back.
IAN: What? After all this trouble. What do you say, Mick?
MICK: I don't know. Sonny's got a point, I guess.
IAN: After all this?
MICK: Well, you give her one. We'll watch.
    (SONNY *and* MICK *laugh.*)
IAN: Hah, hah. Very funny.

EXT. UNDER WAR MEMORIAL IN VILLAGE SQUARE.
NIGHT.
WILLIE BOY *has fallen asleep under the war memorial. He just*
snoozes lightly. Then he wakes with a shiver. He looks across and
sees that the pub is still open. It is late and the lights of the pub are
bright. STEADROY's *music drifts across.*
WILLIE BOY *stands and tries to shake some life back into himself.*

EXT.   OUTSIDE THE PUB.   NIGHT.
BOOTS *is encouraging* FREDRICK *to take another draw of his joint.*
FREDRICK *takes it then looks as though he is turning green. He
stands with help from his sons. The rest of the group are falling about
laughing.*
FREDRICK: I once had some from a fella in the army. It's not
     bad. Quite good.
     (FREDRICK *is being guided, zombie-like, towards his
     Land-Rover.*)
BOOTS: Hey, Freddie! Take a next hit then I want you to break
     dance for me.
     (BOOTS *demonstrates and the laughter increases. His sons
     bundle him into the Land-Rover and everyone watches as it
     begins to move off.*
     WILLIE BOY *comes over and watches with them.*)
BOOTS: Garbo arrive?
WILLIE BOY: Anything wrong with a few minutes of solitary
     peace?
     (WILLIE BOY *turns and walks from them.*)

INT.   BACK ROOM OF PUB.   NIGHT.
WILLIE BOY *comes through into the gloom.* STUART *and* JULIE *are
playing pool.*
WILLIE BOY: You seen Yvette?
     (STUART *stops taking his shot.*)
STUART: I think she went for a walk.
WILLIE BOY: With your friend?
STUART: No, Errol's not with her.
WILLIE BOY: Don't mess me about, you know.
JOHN: (*Comes through into the bar. To* WILLIE BOY) How about
     a drink?
WILLIE BOY: I'll take a whisky. A bottle.
JOHN: A whole bottle?

WILLIE BOY: (*Digging out two five-pound notes and throwing them on the bar*) You don't think I have money?

(STUART *has stopped playing. He just stares at* WILLIE BOY.)

JULIE: Come on, Stuart.

(STUART *takes his shot.* ROBBO *comes through.* JOHN *puts down a bottle of whisky and glass for* WILLIE BOY. *He turns to* ROBBO.)

JOHN: Another glass?

ROBBO: No, man. I must go. (*Pause.*) You all right?

WILLIE BOY: (*Nods*) Just a little tired. I check you tomorrow.

(ROBBO *leaves.* WILLIE BOY *takes another drink and watches* STUART *and* JULIE *playing pool. He is in his own world. He looks set on serious drinking.*)

EXT.   VILLAGE STREET.   NIGHT.

WILLIE BOY *is wandering aimlessly. He stumbles slightly, then corrects himself. Then he walks on. He passes the tavern.* WILLIE BOY *stops. He looks through the window, then he decides to go in. Hold as he disappears through the door.*

INT.   TAVERN.   NIGHT.

WILLIE BOY *walks in. All eyes are unashamedly on him. He momentarily freezes. Then he walks the cat-walk to the bar.*

WILLIE BOY: You have cigarettes?

BARMAN: I'm sorry, sir, I don't understand.

WILLIE BOY: I'm speaking English, aren't I? I said you have any cigarettes?

BARMAN: I see. We have a machine in the lavatories, sir.

WILLIE BOY: Listen. (*He points at the* BARMAN.) I mean you. You have any cigarettes, fella? I want to smoke one while you pull my pint. (*No reaction from the* BARMAN.) You don't have a sense of humour either?

BARMAN: I don't smoke, and it's after hours so I'll have to ask you to leave. I'm afraid I can't sell you any drink.

WILLIE BOY: Okay, okay. Just give me a glass then. (*He puts the whisky on the bar top.*) I have the drink here.

BARMAN: (*Looking around for help now*) Could you please leave, sir, or I shall have no choice but to have you ejected.

44

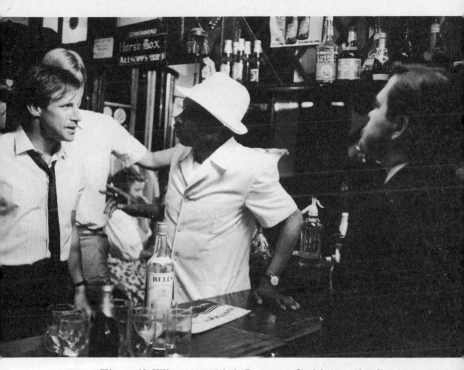

WILLIE BOY: Ejected? What you think I am – a fucking rocket?
(DEREK *and* KEVIN *appear from the throng and signal to the*
BARMAN *that they can take care of him.*)
DEREK: Hello there. Willie, isn't it?
WILLIE BOY: (*Turns around and recognizes him*) Yes, man, you're
the fella from off the coach. Look, if I can't take a drink,
and I can't bum a quick smoke, just tell me one thing. You
see my daughter in here tonight? I can't seem to find her no
place.
DEREK: (*Edging* WILLIE BOY *towards the door*) I'm afraid not.
(*To* KEVIN) And I've been here since eightish, wouldn't you
say?
KEVIN: About that.
WILLIE BOY: Wait. (*He stops.*) Don't push me, man. Don't
push me.
DEREK: Sorry, I didn't mean to push.

45

WILLIE BOY: Listen, man, take your raas clart hands off me, or else I lick you one. (*Takes a drink of whisky*) I gone. I not a cat or dog. You don't have to put me out at night.
(WILLIE BOY *turns and makes a dignified exit. As the door swings back to, the conversation in the tavern becomes more animated.* DEREK *looks at* KEVIN *and shrugs his shoulders.*)

EXT.   VILLAGE STREET OUTSIDE THE TAVERN.   NIGHT.
WILLIE BOY *stands alone. A close-up on his face shows that he has tears in his eyes. He shouts.*
WILLIE BOY: You fuckers! You fuckers you!

INT.   TAVERN.   NIGHT.
All is going on as normal. The BARMAN *is talking to* DEREK *and* KEVIN *about the incident and shaking his head. Through the smoke and civilized chatter of the tavern we can also see that he is pulling both of them pints.*

INT.   BEDROOM.   NIGHT.
VIV *sits in front of the dressing table looking at herself in the mirror. She looks sad, tired and a bit scruffy. She tries to fix her hair. She bends down and takes out her left contact lens and places it in its container. She does the same with the right. She looks back into the mirror and all she sees is an ugly blur.*

INT.   BEDROOM.   NIGHT.
JEFF *sits on the edge of the bed. He is still fully dressed. On the bed is his kitbag and briefcase. He stares at nothing in particular.*

EXT.   BY THE PARISH CHURCH.   NIGHT.
WILLIE BOY *wanders along as if not exactly sure of where it is he is going. He no longer shouts, but he tries to put some purpose into his walking. He takes another swig of the whisky. As he does so he slips and falls over.*
WILLIE BOY: Shit.
(*He stands up and brushes himself off. Then he realizes he's outside the church. He looks over the wall into the graveyard. Then he thinks he can see two people lying moaning in the*

darkness. He tucks the bottle of whisky into his inside jacket
pocket. He climbs the wall and staggers towards them,
increasingly confident with every step. He recognizes ERROL
and shouts as he gets closer.)
WILLIE BOY: You dirty little fucker, I going kill you!
    (ERROL *is making love to* SANDRA. *He turns around and he*
    can now see SANDRA'S *face. He stops and stares at them for a*
    while, then he turns and walks off across the graveyard. ERROL
    moves to get up.)
ERROL: He should be locked up.
    (SANDRA *holds him back.*)
SANDRA: You can't stop now, Errol.

EXT.   GRAVEYARD.   NIGHT.
WILLIE BOY *is sitting down on a tombstone. He takes another drink*
from the whisky and looks up at the stars. Then he puts the bottle to
one side and lies flat on the tombstone. As he goes to pick up the
bottle again he knocks it over. The drink slops out of it.
WILLIE BOY: Jesus Christ.
    (*He closes his eyes. He makes ready to slide into sleep.*
    Pull back off WILLIE BOY *to show the graveyard and*
    eventually the village at night.
    To black.)

EXT.   THE VILLAGE.   MORNING.
The camera gives us a top view of the village. It is sunrise. About
5.30 a.m. The birds are beginning to sing. We hear a cock crow.
In the distance we see a figure walking down an empty road carrying
a bag. He tries to flag down a lone car but it passes him by. There is
no other car in sight.

EXT.   VILLAGE.   SIDE OF THE ROAD.   MORNING.
Later, JEFF *is still standing at the side of the road. He looks around*
feeling uneasy at the silence. He hears a car approaching. JEFF
manages to flag it down. It stops some yards past him. For a few
moments he does nothing as if unable to believe that he has managed
to stop it. Then he picks up his bags and runs after it and gets in. We
watch as the car pulls away.

INT. BEDROOM. MORNING.

YVETTE *is curled up in a chair wide awake. She has obviously not slept all night. She stares out and into space her body tired, her mind working overtime. We can see that she has been crying. In her hand she holds a photo of herself, her mother and Willie Boy.*

INT/EXT. BEDROOM. MORNING.

GODFREY *is standing and looking out of the window. He is just finishing off getting dressed. He encourages the dog to be quiet as it is getting frisky and looks like it might wake up* MARJORIE.

GODFREY *picks up his jacket from the back of a chair. Now he is ready. As he prepares to leave the room* MARJORIE *stirs.*

GODFREY: (*Goes across and kisses her on the forehead*) I won't be long.

   (*She smiles. Both he and the dog leave the room.* MARJORIE *watches as the door closes.*)

INT. CORRIDOR/BEDROOM. MORNING.

GODFREY *stands in the corridor. He is outside the bedroom in which* ERROL *and* STUART *are asleep. He sends the dog downstairs. Then he pushes open the door and peeps around the corner to make sure that both of them are sleeping all right. They are. He gently closes the door as he leaves and turns to go down the stairs.*

EXT. VILLAGE STREET. MORNING.

GODFREY *is striding up a hill. The church bells are pealing. The dog bounds along ahead of him. We see the village* CONSTABLE *riding past on his bicycle.*

CONSTABLE: Morning, Godfrey. Nice day for the game.

GODFREY: Morning, Constable.

   (*The* CONSTABLE *is not sure if it's worth stopping and attempting a conversation. When it becomes clear that* GODFREY *has no intention of stopping, the* CONSTABLE *just presses on his way and weaves down the hill on his bike.*)

EXT. BY THE CHURCH GRAVEYARD. MORNING.

GODFREY *is walking past the church. Suddenly the dog decides to run off and play in the graveyard.*

GODFREY: Polly!
> (*The dog isn't taking any notice.* GODFREY *starts to go into the graveyard himself and fetch the dog. He mutters in annoyance under his breath.*)

EXT. GRAVEYARD. MORNING.
WILLIE BOY *is lying where he lay last night on the tombstone. He opens his eyes. The dog is licking his face. Then behind him he sees* GODFREY *looking down.* WILLIE BOY *starts to try and sit up. He has a huge hangover and his body feels as stiff and crumpled as he looks.*
WILLIE BOY: I don't remember a blasted thing.
> (GODFREY *taps the empty whisky bottle with his walking stick. He reaches down to give him a hand.*)
GODFREY: One doesn't.
> (WILLIE BOY *sits up straight.*)

INT. CHURCH. MORNING.

The congregation are belting forth a hymn. MISS RYE *plays the organ. The West Indian team look shabby and rather depleted.* ROBBO *glances at the spare places on the pew and arches his eyebrows to* LOUIS, *who simply shrugs his shoulders.* ERROL *gives up the hymn and slumps back to his seat, head in hands.* JULIE *looks across at the West Indians.* SANDRA *doesn't turn her head.*

SANDRA: So you didn't then?

JULIE: He wouldn't.

> (MARJORIE *is singing too loud.* FREDRICK *holds out an open palm.* TOMMY, *the elder son, places two paracetamol in it.*)

INT. KITCHEN. MORNING.

WILLIE BOY *is sitting at the kitchen table finishing off breakfast.* GODFREY *is fussing about making coffee. He brings the two cups to the table.*

GODFREY: Had enough?

WILLIE BOY: Plenty, man. Plenty.

GODFREY: (*Points to a pile of letters he has dug out*) You know what these are?

WILLIE BOY: Letters?

GODFREY: These are the people I live with in my dreams.

WILLIE BOY: You read over your old letters?

(GODFREY *begins to clear off the things from the breakfast table.*)

GODFREY: Of course. (*Pause.*) Do you have letters?

WILLIE BOY: Gas bill, electricity bill, telephone bill, rates bill.

GODFREY: No continental communication?

WILLIE BOY: Not really. Only from Mildred, my wife who's back home checking out the scene.

GODFREY: I see now why you end up in graveyards. (*He continues to clear up.*)

WILLIE BOY: Wait. You think there's something wrong with me? I simply had a little liquor and I fall down dead drunk. Seems to me a perfectly normal way of carrying on for a fella on a Saturday night.

(GODFREY *looks askance at him.*)

All right, maybe I had in a little bit more liquor than I would normally. But I lost my daughter. I was under pressure, man.

GODFREY: You don't have to justify anything to me.

WILLIE BOY: Well, you sure making me feel like I do.

GODFREY: (*Laughs*) Me? A man who cuts roses and misses the occasional bout of dysentery? (*Pause. Almost secretively*) Remember when you were a child and you had a secret place, a place you always liked to go where you knew nobody could find you?

WILLIE BOY: Sure man, I used to hide in a cave by Cockleshell beach and cover the entrance with leaves from the coconut tree.

GODFREY: Well, I don't think I can manage anything that exotic, but I'll show you my adult – or ancient – equivalent. It's not a secret, exactly, but it serves the same purpose.

51

INT. SNOOKER ROOM. MORNING.

GODFREY *peels back the covering from off the snooker table. It is a precise ritual.*

GODFREY: You have played snooker before?

WILLIE BOY: Just once. I'm not very good.

(GODFREY *racks up the balls and prepares to break.*)

GODFREY: Standard of play is irrelevant. The rules are of paramount importance. As long as you know the rules. (*He takes the opening shot and breaks up the pack of reds.*)

EXT. CHURCH. MORNING.

Long shot of everyone pouring out of church at the end of the service. The VICAR *is there doing the shaking of hands bit.*

MISS RYE *is leaning against her bike and looking to see if she can see* WILLIE BOY. *She cannot. Clearly she is not going to ask anyone where he is, but she is worried.*

EXT. VILLAGE LANE. MORNING.

ROBBO, LOUIS, DESERT HEAD, WILF, STEADROY *and* BOOTS *are walking away from the church.* PAT *and* MASIE *and* YVETTE *follow separately, as do* STUART *and* ERROL.

ROBBO: Well, I suppose if Willie Boy don't show I better take the captain's role.

(BOOTS *sucks his teeth. Nobody says anything. They walk on.*)

STEADROY: (*To* ROBBO) So what we going do about no Jeff?

ROBBO: Seems like he don't want to be around black people anymore.

STEADROY: But even if Willie Boy show up we have only nine players.

BOOTS: You going play twice, Robbo?

(DESERT HEAD *laughs.* ROBBO *throws him a sharp look. They walk on.*)

EXT. BY A STREAM. MORNING.

LOUIS, BOOTS, STEADROY, ROBBO, WILF *and* DESERT HEAD *are all down a muddy embankment taking a piss into a stream.*

LOUIS: (*Zipping himself up*) Listen, why we don't just call off the game, eh?

BOOTS: I second that. I don't want to play, in truth.
STEADROY: Nor me.
  (ROBBO *has finished. He gives them a contemptuous glance then
  starts to climb back up to the road.*)
DESERT HEAD: Man, I'm hungry. I could eat a cow.
  (*They all look at* DESERT HEAD *contemptuously.*)

INT. SNOOKER ROOM. MORNING.
GODFREY *is practically clearing the table on his own.* WILLIE BOY
is sitting patting the dog.
We hear MARJORIE *shout 'Godfrey'.* GODFREY *stops playing and
looks at* WILLIE BOY, *as though telling him to be quiet.*

INT. HALLWAY. MORNING.
A nervous-looking MARJORIE *stands in the hallway. Having
returned from church she is now ready to leave for the cricket. She*

knows where GODFREY *is, but she also knows that she cannot disturb him. She calls once more.*
MARJORIE: Godfrey! It's after twelve, Godfrey.
　　(*She turns to leave.*)

INT.　SNOOKER ROOM.　MORNING.
We hear the front door slam shut. GODFREY *pots a ball, puts down the cue, and turns to* WILLIE BOY.
GODFREY: We had better go now.

EXT.　VILLAGE GREEN.　AFTERNOON.
MARJORIE *is passing around sandwiches.*
JOHN *has set up his bar under the open-fronted marquee and everyone seems more interested in drinking than listening to* DEREK. *A frustrated* DEREK *flourishes his team sheet.*
DEREK: (*Shouts*) Can all the team players register with me first?

JOHN: (*Sarcastic*) Do you want me to stick up a notice?
DEREK: (*Caustic*) No, thank you.
VIV: (*Points*) Oh look, Derek. There's a couple more cars
  arriving.
  (*In the middle distance we see Fredrick's Land-Rover and
  another car approaching in convoy.*)
DEREK: Well, that's it then. All present and correct.

EXT.   PAVILION ON VILLAGE GREEN.   AFTERNOON.
*The Brixton team have been supplied with a few trays of neat
sandwiches and some jugs of orange juice. They seem uninterested.
Only* STEADROY's *music lightens the gloom.* ERROL *lies flat out
asleep.* YVETTE *is sitting quietly with* MASIE *and* PAT. *She is
clearly upset because of the disappearance of her father.* ROBBO *has
a piece of paper and a pen in his hand.*
DESERT HEAD: Where's the roast beef and Suffolk pudding?
WILF: (*Fingering a piece of bread*) We the ones who are going to
  need famine relief.
ROBBO: (*To the whole team*) Well, we going to play the game or
  not?
LOUIS: (*Looking across at the village team*) Maybe one of them
  seen Willie Boy?
BOOTS: I done already ask. Nobody seen him since he sat like a
  pigeon in the square.
ROBBO: (*Exasperated by their lack of initiative*) We just wait
  then?
  (*Nobody replies.* DEREK *comes over. He is bouncing a ball up
  in the air on a bat.*)
DEREK: Well, ready when you are. You chaps seem a bit short.
BOOTS: Yeah, we all fell in a puddle and shrunk.
  (DEREK *laughs alone.*)
YVETTE: (*Points and shouts*) Look, there he is!

EXT.   VILLAGE GREEN.   AFTERNOON.
WILLIE BOY *and* GODFREY *are walking quite casually across the
grass towards us. The dog is running free.*
We track YVETTE *as she runs towards her father. She thuds into his
arms.* GODFREY *seems pleased, but he continues to walk.*

55

WILLIE BOY: Child, where have you been?

YVETTE: Nowhere.

WILLIE BOY: What you mean nowhere? Who you been with?

(YVETTE *unpeels herself from her father and stands facing him.*)

YVETTE: I've been with nobody, Dad. Nobody.

(*Hold as they look at each other.*)

Dad, I don't want to go on like this anymore. We should be with Mum. Please? Let's try it. Call it a holiday if you like, but we're growing apart.

WILLIE BOY: Growing apart?

YVETTE: We're driving each other mad without even realizing. And there's Mum.

(WILLIE BOY *stares at his daughter, then he hugs her.*)

WILLIE BOY: Later, sweetheart. Just let me deal with this, then we'll talk later. I promise.

EXT. PAVILION. AFTERNOON.

GODFREY *is picking up the stumps and balls and bails, etc. from a bag. He strains his back as he bends to do so. Then he straightens up and pats his dog on the head.*

MARJORIE *is watching him. He starts to walk off. She comes to him.*

MARJORIE: (*In a quiet voice*) Godfrey?

GODFREY: In a moment, dear. The game.

(*He walks on at his own slow pace towards the wicket. The dog remains with* MARJORIE.)

EXT. PAVILION. AFTERNOON.

DEREK *has the attention of most of his team.*

DEREK: Well, let's play hard but fair, with passion and the basics uppermost in our mind. Remember, keep your eye on the ball. It's as simple as that. Now then, how's the head, Fredrick?

FREDRICK: Nothing a couple of pints and some swift batting can't fix.

EXT. PAVILION. AFTERNOON.

WILLIE BOY *comes out of the pavilion. He has now changed into his whites.* ROBBO *is by his side. They come towards the team.* ERROL *has on a Walkman.* STEADROY *still plays some sounds from his cassette player.*

ROBBO: Although we only have nine men, Willie Boy still thinks we should go ahead.

WILLIE BOY: Pat, you can play?

LOUIS: No, man, it can't go so.

WILLIE BOY: I'm only asking if she can play.

PAT: I don't want to play.

BOOTS: It don't look good with a woman anyhow.

LOUIS: Pat, you ever play?

PAT: I don't want to play, that's all. (*To* WILLIE BOY) Why you don't ask Masie or Yvette?

YVETTE: I don't want to either.

WILLIE BOY: Masie?

MASIE: I'll try.

BOOTS: Jesus Christ.

LOUIS: You can play?

WILLIE BOY: It doesn't matter. She can catch a ball and throw it.

STEADROY: (*Hardly pausing from music*) The sister have a right to play.

BOOTS: This equality shit gone too far, man. (*He gets up and walks off.*)

STEADROY: (*Watching him go*) He soon come. He can't go no place.

WILLIE BOY: I don't have no big speech or team talk or nothing to give. Everybody have their own ideas about what we doing here and whether we should be here and all the rest. But now we here we might as well play. And I mean play. I don't have no time to make joke with these people. A cricket field don't be no place to separate the good from the bad; it's us and them. No gentlemen shit out there. We play, we win, and we gone. But most of all we win, you hear?

(*Nobody says anything. They just look at* WILLIE BOY. *Pause and hold.*)

57

EXT. WICKET. AFTERNOON.
Three heads are in the frame. GODFREY, DEREK *and* WILLIE
BOY. GODFREY *looks at them both then tosses the coin.*

EXT. WICKET. AFTERNOON.
*A fifty-pence coin lies on the grass. The head of Queen Elizabeth II
is visible.*

EXT. WICKET. AFTERNOON.
Three heads are in the frame. GODFREY *turns to* DEREK.
DEREK: We'll bat first.
    (WILLIE BOY *nods.* DEREK *proffers his hand.* WILLIE BOY
    shakes it.)

EXT. PAVILION. AFTERNOON.
*The Brixton team are limbering up and about to trot out on to the
pitch.* STUART *has taken the gloves and pads to keep wicket, and*
BOOTS *is throwing the ball at him for practice.*
WILLIE BOY: Robbo, you still feel good to bowl?
ROBBO: You think I over the hill or what?
WILLIE BOY: (*To* DESERT HEAD) You want to open as well?
    (DESERT HEAD *looks up.*)
DESERT HEAD: Sure, man. You want me bowl anything in
    particular?
WILLIE BOY: Just the ball.
STEADROY: (*Dry*) Cho, man, a next Lenny Henry talking.
WILLIE BOY: (*To* MASIE) When you get it just throw it at
    Stuart.
MASIE: Is that all?
WILLIE BOY: I'll tell you as we go along.
    (WILLIE BOY *turns to* YVETTE *and* PAT, *who will be left on
    their own. He picks up the scorebook from out of the kit bag.*)
WILLIE BOY: Either one of you know how to keep a scorebook?
PAT: A what?
WILLIE BOY: No, it doesn't matter. (*He shouts at* STEADROY.)
    Hey, you look like you going to sleep, man.
    (STEADROY *opens his eyes and stands up. He picks up his
    cassette player.*)

59

WILLIE BOY: Leave it, man. You can't play and listen to music at the same time.

PAT: We'll listen to it.

STEADROY: (*Shrugs his shoulders*) Okay, but watch it good.

> (STEADROY *ambles off.* WILLIE BOY *turns to go.* PAT *turns up the music.* VIV *comes across as* PAT *and* YVETTE *watch* WILLIE BOY *running into the distance.*
>
> *She begins to gather up the empty plates, and the half-empty jugs of orange juice. She smiles as if she is going to say something, but she does not. Instead she gets on with her gathering up.*)

EXT.   PAVILION.   AFTERNOON.

MARJORIE, *who is sitting with other people, looks across at* VIV *gathering up the things, and the two black women sitting on the grass listening to music. Then she looks away guiltily. Like* VIV *she too wants to begin the 'girls' talk', but she is not sure how to.*

EXT.   IN FRONT OF PAVILION.   AFTERNOON.

The first two men in the village team are padded up. One is the VICAR, *the other is* JOHN.

VICAR: Good, well, I think we're just about ready.

MICK: Said your prayers, Vicar? These blokes can bowl a bit.

VICAR: It's only a friendly, Michael. I don't think we'll be needing to call upon the arbitrary powers of the Good Lord.

> (DEREK *is standing by the scoreboard keeper who we recognize as the* BARMAN *from the tavern.*)

DEREK: A nice solid platform to the innings if you can manage it. No heroics, eh?

> (*The two batsmen begin to walk out towards the wicket.* FREDRICK *shouts after them.*)

FREDRICK: Here, Vicar, you forgot your helmet.

VICAR: (*Stops and looks back with concern*) Helmet?

> (*Fredrick's group all burst out into helpless laughter. The* VICAR *still does not understand.*)

EXT.   WICKET.   AFTERNOON.

Wide shot of the wicket. The VICAR *is about to face the first ball.* GODFREY *is the umpire. The square leg umpire is the* COLONEL.

DESERT HEAD *is about to bowl the first ball. He has an*
exaggeratedly long run up. WILLIE BOY *signals to him to wait a*
minute while he makes some final adjustments to the field placings.
Now he is ready.

EXT. WICKET. AFTERNOON.
Close-up of DESERT HEAD's *foot. Like a bull he is tearing at the*
grass and cutting a mark.

EXT. PAVILION. AFTERNOON.
FREDRICK *looks at* MICK *as if to say 'Bloody hell, what's this?'*

EXT. WICKET. AFTERNOON.
In close-up DESERT HEAD *now rubs the ball against his crotch. He*
is shining it up.

EXT. PAVILION. AFTERNOON.
MARJORIE *and* VIV *look on.* MARJORIE *is slightly embarrassed by*
what is going on and her cup of tea rattles ominously against her
saucer. VIV *notices* MARJORIE's *unease but says nothing.*

EXT. WICKET. AFTERNOON.
We have a close-up of the VICAR's *face as he prepares to face this*
first ball. He is a picture of concern.

EXT. WICKET. AFTERNOON.
DESERT HEAD *gives the ball a final rub. There is no trace of a smile*
on his face as we track him loping in to deliver the first ball.
The VICAR *offers a wild stroke, but the ball is wide.*
STUART *dives to his right to collect behind the stumps.*
The VICAR *looks relieved that this initial confrontation is over.*

EXT. WICKET. AFTERNOON.
GODFREY *turns towards the pavilion and signals the ball as a wide.*

EXT. WICKET. AFTERNOON.
Behind the stumps members of the Brixton side just shake their
heads.

ROBBO: (*1st slip*) Ganja mess up his vision.
BOOTS: (*2nd slip*) Just play the game, man. The bowler is
    allowed a loosener.

EXT. PAVILION. AFTERNOON.
The scoreboard man ceremoniously marks up the first run for
Sneddington on the scoreboard.
CONSTABLE: I can only count ten of them.
FREDRICK: Maybe they got hungry and ate the other one last
    night.
    (*Nearly all of them laugh or pretend to be amused, except*
    MARJORIE *and* VIV. *We hear the sound of leather on willow*
    and cut back.)

EXT. WICKET. AFTERNOON.
The VICAR *has scored a couple of runs and the two batsmen are*
scurrying between the wicket. There is organized panic in the Brixton
outfield, but the ball comes back swiftly to STUART.
We hear the VICAR *being applauded from the side lines and he raises*
his bat as if he has scored a fifty.

EXT. PAVILION. AFTERNOON.
They continue to applaud the VICAR.
DEREK: Well, it seems as though the Vicar said his prayers this
    morning.
FREDRICK: (*Pouring a pint*) Well, he bloody better keep saying
    them if he's going to stay out there.
    (*The man on the scoreboard is changing it to indicate that the*
    VICAR *has just scored two runs.*)

EXT. WICKET. AFTERNOON.
A little time has passed. ROBBO *is now preparing to bowl to* JOHN.
The field is much the same as it was for DESERT HEAD. GODFREY
is still umpiring at the wicket. Camera tracks ROBBO *running in to*
bowl to JOHN.
He gets him LBW. The whole West Indian team leaps and appeals.
ROBBO *swivels around to face* GODFREY.

EXT. WICKET. AFTERNOON.
Close up on GODFREY *who has no hesitation in raising his finger
and signalling* JOHN *out.*

EXT. WICKET. AFTERNOON.
Wider shot. JOHN *begins to walk. He has to pass* GODFREY *and the*
VICAR *on his way from the field.*
VICAR: Bad luck there, John. Very close.
JOHN: (*Under his breath as he passes by* GODFREY) Bastard.
VICAR: I say. There was no need for that.
    (*The West Indians are celebrating and slapping hands, etc.*
    ROBBO *is the hero of the moment.*)

EXT. PAVILION. AFTERNOON.
We pick JOHN *up and track him as he crosses the next batsman in,
who is the* CONSTABLE.
CONSTABLE: Bad luck.
    (JOHN *ignores him. As he reaches the boundary he tears off his
    gloves and throws them on the ground.*)
FREDRICK: Godfrey getting a suntan out there, is he?
JOHN: If that's how they play no wonder they win all the bloody
    time.
DEREK: (*Looking in the direction of the scoreboard. He is smoking a
    pipe.*) Nineteen for one. It's not a bad start. Not a bad start
    at all.

EXT. PAVILION. AFTERNOON.
*Later. Close up on the scoreboard. We see it is 103 for 8. We hear
leather on willow.*

EXT. WICKET. AFTERNOON.
DEREK *is at the crease. At the other end of the wicket is* TOMMY.
*The field is tighter, which suggests that the West Indians have got on
top a little bit.*

EXT. WICKET. AFTERNOON.
ERROL *is preparing to bowl. He is rubbing the ball vigorously in his
crotch, trying to put some shine back on it.*

EXT. PAVILION. AFTERNOON.
The Sneddington team are standing and drinking, too much perhaps.
IAN: Looks like he's trying to rub his balls off.
MICK: Sandra probably did that for him last night.
   (*They all laugh.*)
IAN: Someone better start pouring Derek a drink.

EXT. WICKET. AFTERNOON.
We track ERROL *as he now begins to come in to bowl, head down,
working up some pace.*

EXT. WICKET. AFTERNOON.
We see DEREK's *face as he prepares to receive. He seems not entirely
sure of what he's doing. He swings wildly and the ball goes high off
the top edge.*
We see MASIE *teetering underneath the ball.*
WILLIE BOY: Girl, catch it! Catch it!
   (MASIE *takes a very good catch and a huge roar goes up from
   the West Indian team and they all run to hug her up. Even*
   BOOTS *and* LOUIS *laugh with delight.*)

EXT. PAVILION. AFTERNOON.
YVETTE *is laid flat out on the grass. The music from* STEADROY's
cassette player is still playing. Without turning around PAT *speaks to*
YVETTE.
PAT: She take it. She take the catch!
   (*She gets no answer. Then she turns around and realizes that*
   YVETTE *is fast asleep. She seems peaceful.* MARJORIE *looks
   across and applauds.* PAT *looks back at her.*)

EXT. PAVILION. AFTERNOON.
DEREK *walks in and crosses the next batsman,* SONNY, *who
murmurs 'Prat' under his breath as he goes by.* DEREK *falters a
moment then just carries on walking. When he reaches the boundary
there are a few 'hard lucks' but the spirit seems to have gone out of
the side.* DEREK *looks at the scoreboard. The man changes it to 103
for 9.* DEREK *begins to take off his pads.* VIV *comes across and gives
him a maternal hug.*

64

VIV: Don't worry, darling.

IAN: Another captain's innings from you, Derek. Nought
again.

DEREK: Well, I did hear they were a better bowling side than
they were batting.

FREDRICK: You heard what? Did you also hear how they like to
get pissed and run amok in our village?

DEREK: I don't think there's any need for that sort of talk,
especially in front of the ladies.

VICAR: I quite agree and, if you don't mind my saying, people
in glass houses shouldn't throw stones.

*(The uneasiness between those in Fredrick's marquee-orientated
camp and those in Derek's and the Vicar's has grown.*

*Cut back to wicket falling and the West Indians shouting in
delight. Everyone in the village team just looks at each other but
says nothing.)*

VIV: Look, they're coming off.

(DEREK looks at her.)

EXT. WICKET. AFTERNOON.

*The two village batsmen, TOMMY and SONNY, are coming off to a
trickle of applause from the West Indians. The dog has broken away
from MARJORIE and begins to race across the field towards
GODFREY.*

*TOMMY and SONNY arrive. They sit down and begin to unpad
without saying anything.*

FREDRICK: *(Sarcastic)* Brilliant team performance.

KEVIN: Yes, your three runs were a great help.

(FREDRICK looks sharply at him.

WILLIE BOY comes across to the Sneddington camp.)

WILLIE BOY: *(To DEREK)* Straight around, or you want to have
a tea break or something?

(DEREK turns and looks to his team-mates.)

FREDRICK: *(Without looking up at WILLIE BOY)* Straight
around.

EXT. WICKET. AFTERNOON.

Medium shot of GODFREY standing in the middle of the field eating

biscuits and throwing tit-bits to his dog. He is encouraging the dog to jump and catch bits. When it does he pats it.

EXT. PAVILION. AFTERNOON.
MARJORIE *stares out at* GODFREY. *She seems sad and undecided as to whether to go and join him out there or stay where she is.*

EXT. PAVILION. AFTERNOON.
WILLIE BOY *comes back and looks around.* WILF *and* BOOTS *are padding up.* STUART *is sitting with* ERROL *who has on his Walkman.* YVETTE *is sleeping still.* STEADROY *has reclaimed his music and is lying on the grass.*
WILLIE BOY: We going straight round. I don't want no wild shit. Play steady and we got them under control. You two ready?
(WILF *and* BOOTS *nod.*)

Okay then, let's go.

ERROL: (*With Walkman still on*) Viv Richards finish?

DESERT HEAD: Viv Richards! (*Laughs.*)

(WILLIE BOY *looks at them both and sucks his teeth.*)

EXT. WICKET. AFTERNOON.
A wide shot of the wicket. WILF *is at the crease.* BOOTS *is at the other end.* DEREK *has set an attacking field.* KEVIN *is all set to open the bowling. We track* KEVIN *as he comes in quickly and* WILF *snicks the ball away for a single. They run one, and then realize there has been a misfield by* FREDRICK. *In their panic they manage to make it back for a second run.*

EXT. PAVILION. AFTERNOON.
Scoreboard. The man is changing it to 2 for 0.

EXT. PAVILION. AFTERNOON.
The West Indians on the boundary begin to cheer their encouragement.

LOUIS: I didn't realize Wilf can run so!

ROBBO: I think he's just pleased to take a next run off the fat bastard.

WILLIE BOY: We keep this up we'll be through in forty minutes.

EXT. VILLAGE GREEN. AFTERNOON.
Later. We have a medium shot of SANDRA *and* JULIE *walking towards the Sneddington group. They stop and look out towards the wicket at the game. As they watch there is a shout, as if a wicket has fallen.*

EXT. PAVILION. AFTERNOON.
We hold on the scoreboard which is now being changed to '18 for 4'.

EXT. WICKET. AFTERNOON.
The stumps are uprooted. KEVIN *is overjoyed.* DEREK *rushes forward to join him, and a beaming* VICAR *makes his way across to them.*

EXT. PAVILION. AFTERNOON.

ROBBO *has arrived back dejected. He looks at* ERROL.

ROBBO: Do what you can. You're the last hope.

(ERROL *just nods at him and walks off.* ROBBO *throws his bat down by the boundary.*)

ROBBO: They're not bad.

PAT: You only made four.

STEADROY: And the way you standing I sure you going to be stumped.

ROBBO: (*Sharply*) So I'm not Sobers. (*He sits down.*)

LOUIS: Don't worry man, nobody seriously vex with you.

ROBBO: I know that but like Willie Boy I can't stand the idea of losing to these people.

EXT. WICKET. AFTERNOON.

Wide shot of the wicket. ERROL *faces his first delivery from* KEVIN *and hits it for a straight four. He does not even bother to run.* WILLIE BOY *who is at the other end gives him 'thumbs up'.*

EXT. VILLAGE GREEN. AFTERNOON.

SANDRA *and* JULIE *look on.* JULIE *nudges* SANDRA *who smiles.*

EXT. WICKET. AFTERNOON.

Later. KEVIN *is standing on his own. The ball is thrown back to him. He catches it in one hand and then begins to shine it vigorously on the seat of his pants. He looks all around and then, with great determination, he begins to run up. We track him as he comes in with maximum effort and delivers the ball.*

ERROL *tries to drive and is dropped behind by the* CONSTABLE.

KEVIN: (*Looks skyward and shouts*) For Christ's sake, what's the matter with this team?

FREDRICK: (*In slips*) We have to play with stuck up little twats like you, that's what's the matter. (*To* CONSTABLE) Hard luck, pal.

(KEVIN *turns on* FREDRICK *and begins to march towards him.* FREDRICK *squares up to meet him.* DEREK *comes rushing in from the covers and stands in between them.*)

DEREK: Okay, any argument and you'll have to leave the field
and sort it out.

KEVIN: This bloody useless lout can't talk to me like that. I'm
sorry, Derek, but he has to be taught a lesson.

FREDRICK: Not by a fucking poof like you.

(DEREK *holds back* KEVIN. GODFREY *sees what is going on
and turns away. He looks out to the scoreboard.*)

EXT. PAVILION. AFTERNOON.
*On the scoreboard, Errol is 24, Willie Boy is on 9. The team is on
51 for 4, chasing 103.*

EXT. PAVILION. AFTERNOON.
*The West Indians on the boundary have noticed that something is
happening on the field of play.*

69

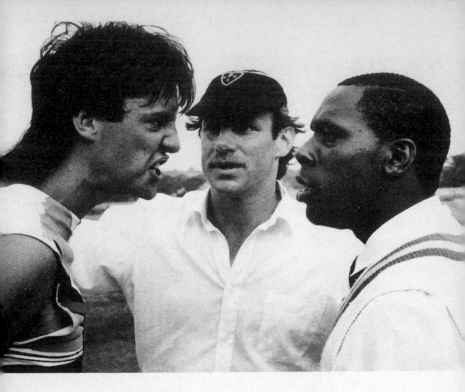

ROBBO: Look like a commotion of some kind.

EXT. PAVILION. AFTERNOON.
MARJORIE *sits with the dog. She is feeling increasingly
uncomfortable.*

EXT. WICKET. AFTERNOON.
Later. IAN *is bowling spin off a short run to* ERROL. *He comes in to
bowl and there is a huge shout for LBW. He turns quickly to look at*
GODFREY.

EXT. WICKET. AFTERNOON.
Close up on GODFREY. *He does not move or give any signal.*

EXT. WICKET. AFTERNOON.
IAN *turns to* ERROL.

IAN: Oh, for Christ's sake!

ERROL: For Christ's sake what?

IAN: You can walk, you know. Or do you lot always cheat?

ERROL: Who the fuck are you calling cheat?

(DEREK *comes racing across.*)

DEREK: Please, let's just carry on with the game.

IAN: Either that cheating bastard is out or I go. It was plum LBW.

DEREK: Oh come on, Ian, it's a game that's all.

(*He hands* IAN *the ball. After a pause* IAN *takes it and walks away.* DEREK *is left standing uncomfortably on his own.*)

EXT. PAVILION. AFTERNOON.
Most of the team are standing and looking out to the wicket.

STEADROY: Seem like pressure reach.

LOUIS: If the umpire give him not out then he's not out. They expect a big man like him to walk?

EXT. PAVILION. AFTERNOON.
On the scoreboard we can see that it is now 75 for 4.
ERROL *is on 42, Willie Boy 15.*

EXT. WICKET. AFTERNOON.
Wider shot of the wicket as IAN *comes in to bowl his spin to* ERROL *again. Again* ERROL *plays forward and the ball thumps his pad.*
IAN *jumps up and turns around to face* GODFREY.

IAN: Owzat!

(GODFREY *says nothing. He simply indicates with the slightest of movements that the ball was going down the leg side.*)

IAN: You've got to be bloody joking. Are they paying you? Or is this one of your missus' ploys to be nice to the darkies? Well? Is it?

GODFREY: (*Looking hard at him*) The rules of the game say I determine whether or not the batsman is out. In this case the batsman is not out.

IAN: (*In disbelief*) Bloody hell!

(IAN *turns away from* GODFREY *and walks towards* ERROL. ERROL *stands, seemingly unconcerned, practising his guard.*)

72

IAN: (*To* ERROL) Well, are you going to play the game or not?
DEREK: (*Comes over from the covers again.*) Oh, come on, Ian.
SANDRA: (*Shouts from boundary*) He's not out!
IAN: (*Looks at her, then back at* ERROL) Well?
  (ERROL *ignores him. He demonstrates a cover drive, then
  waves at* SANDRA.)
IAN: Right. That's it.
  (*He turns to go.* FREDRICK *shouts after him.*)
FREDRICK: Hold on, Ian. I'm on my way as well. (*He addresses
  his sons.*)
  Come on, lads.
DAVID: But, Dad, you can't just . . .
  (FREDRICK *cuffs him around the head.* IAN, FREDRICK,
  TOMMY *and* DAVID *begin to leave the field. They are
  immediately joined by* SONNY *and* MICK. *There are just five
  members of the Sneddington team left.*
  GODFREY *stands impassively.* DEREK *looks speechless.*)

EXT. PAVILION. AFTERNOON.
There is astonishment among the Brixton team.
YVETTE: Maybe one of them has to change their nappy.
LOUIS: All of them by the look of it.
WILF: What happens now?
  (*Nobody says anything.*)

EXT. WICKET. AFTERNOON.
DEREK *stands in the middle of the wicket alone. He has just watched
them leave the field. He turns to* GODFREY.
DEREK: Well, if it's all right we'll just carry on.
  (GODFREY *says nothing. The* VICAR, CONSTABLE, KEVIN
  and JOHN *are all that are left.* DEREK *turns to them.*)
  Vicar, maybe you can keep wicket. Kevin – bowl. The rest
  of us just spread out as best we can.
  (*The absurdity of it seems to have struck everyone except*
  DEREK.)

EXT. PAVILION. AFTERNOON.
FREDRICK *and sons are climbing into the Land-Rover. The lads are*

73

getting on to their motorbikes. SANDRA *and* JULIE *have made their way around the boundary.*

SANDRA: What's the matter with you lot then?

MICK: Ask your boyfriend.

JULIE: Won't they let you play?

IAN: Piss off.

> (*They begin to move off.*)

SANDRA: Charming bunch of pigs, aren't they.

EXT. WICKET. AFTERNOON.

From DEREK's *POV he watches as they start to drive off. His eyes track them for a little while.*

EXT. PAVILION. AFTERNOON.

The West Indians are also looking as they begin to circle the village green and move away out of sight. Then LOUIS *looks back at the wicket.*

LOUIS: You mean to tell me these fellers really going to carry on with just five players?

> (*Nobody says anything as it is self-evidently true.*)

EXT. WICKET. AFTERNOON.

We have a medium shot of the wicket. We can see that ERROL *is facing* KEVIN. *He meets the ball on the up and cuts it cleanly for four. He does not bother to run. Neither do any of the fielders as it would be a futile chase.*

EXT. WICKET. AFTERNOON.

We have a tighter shot of ERROL, *leaning confidently against his bat. Then he walks to the mid-wicket area to talk with* WILLIE BOY *who has drifted down to meet him.*

ERROL: You think we should give them a chance and stretch it out a bit?

WILLIE BOY: Do what?

ERROL: Make a game of it.

WILLIE BOY: The thing I always notice about you, youth, is how you like to shape tough for the white man, but you don't really know how to deal with him, do you?

ERROL: I'm just talking about making a game of it.
WILLIE BOY: You make me laugh, you know. (*He walks off.*)
  (ERROL *shrugs his shoulders. It was the end of the over.*
  WILLIE BOY *goes back to the crease where it is his turn to take
  up the strike. He looks up.*
  DEREK *comes in to bowl off a short run. The ball comes down
  the wicket. It is loose and* WILLIE BOY *hits it for a straight six.
  As everybody else follows the ball,* WILLIE BOY *throws a hard
  look down the wicket towards* ERROL.
  ERROL *can't stop himself as he starts to smile.*)

EXT. PAVILION. AFTERNOON.
MARJORIE *and* VIV *sit together watching the game.*
MARJORIE: (*Touches* VIV's *arm*) I feel desperate for Derek.
  (VIV *smiles gratefully.* SANDRA *and* JULIE *stand by the
  pavilion and look out at the field of play.*)

75

JULIE: Will you see him again?

SANDRA: I've got his address. He said to ring him when I come to London.

JULIE: You've never been to London.

SANDRA: I know.

(*Tighten into* SANDRA. *Hold.*)

EXT. PAVILION. AFTERNOON.

Later. The atmosphere is becoming decidedly more lethargic.

ROBBO: How many we need now?

BOOTS: Just three more.

WILF: (*Looking at scorebook*) Errol's made the fastest fifty since we started keeping a book.

(*We hear the sound of a ball being struck.*)

ROBBO: You better add four to his score for that's it.

YVETTE: (*Getting to her feet*) Is it finished?

PAT: It's finished.

EXT. VILLAGE GREEN. AFTERNOON.

ERROL *and* WILLIE BOY *are walking off with the five Sneddington players applauding them. 'Well done!', etc.*

GODFREY *walks behind with the stumps.*

EXT. PAVILION. AFTERNOON.

MARJORIE *watches everyone trooping off. She gets to her feet and frees the dog. It romps off towards* GODFREY. VIV *gets to her feet, too.* SANDRA *and* JULIE *stand watching everyone coming off.*

JULIE: Are you gonna say anything to him?

SANDRA: He's busy. (*Pause.*) I'll write to him.

EXT. PAVILION. AFTERNOON.

PAT *and* MASIE *begin to clear up loose jumpers, papers, plates, etc.*

WILLIE BOY: (*To* ERROL) So you save your best form for the end of the season.

ERROL: I can't think of no better time.

(WILLIE BOY *offers his hand.* ERROL *shakes it.*)

STEADROY: So what now? We can go? We get a trophy or something?

(WILLIE BOY *looks across to where* MARJORIE *is standing.*

DEREK, KEVIN, VICAR, JOHN *and the* CONSTABLE,
plus VIV, *are grouped around her.*
MARJORIE *takes out a piece of paper.* SANDRA *and* JULIE,
and the few other spectators, have closed in. GODFREY *and the
dog stand close by.*
DEREK *notices the West Indians' reluctance to come over.*)

DEREK: Could we all possibly gather around. Marjorie would
like to say a few words of congratulations.
(WILLIE BOY *turns to the others and leads them the few yards
or so towards* MARJORIE.
A tight shot of MARJORIE *as she tentatively begins to make this
prepared and pre-rehearsed speech.*)

MARJORIE: Ladies and gentlemen of Sneddington Cricket Club,
guests, spectators. I'd firstly like to thank all the men
concerned for a thrilling game of cricket. In the end it
mattered little who won, we were all entertained.
(*Tighter shot of* GODFREY *who listens to her speech, as if he
would like to help in some way. He knows she is struggling.*)
(*Continuing. Pause.*) I'd especially like to thank the men,
and women, of Brixton Conquistadors XI for giving up
their time to be here with us this weekend.
(*People tentatively applaud. There is a cavernous pause, as if*
MARJORIE *is missing out some of the speech. Her eyes roam
across the words. Then she swallows and begins again. She lifts
her head from the prepared speech. She has given up with the
text – improvising in order to reach a swift conclusion.*)
It's a terribly long way for people to come to play a game of
cricket, but we are grateful for the effort and look forward
to having you back again. Thank you very much for the
marvellous contribution you've made.
(*Healthier and more confident applause.* MARJORIE *comes
forward to shake hands with* WILLIE BOY. DEREK *does the
same. We see* GODFREY *slip his arm around* MARJORIE'S
*shoulders. She looks up at him happy for his warmth and
support at this moment.*)

DEREK: (*Smiles bravely*) Maybe next year we'll come to you.
(*Laughs*) With a full contingent.

BOOTS: And this time we going make the bet.

EXT. VILLAGE GREEN. EARLY EVENING.
The team have now got on the coach. ROBBO *stands with* WILLIE
BOY, *who is looking back across the village green.*
WILLIE BOY: You'd think the least they could have done was
offer us a drink at the pub, or something.
ROBBO: But these people got their difficulties, man.
WILLIE BOY: And you don't think we got ours?
(ROBBO *looks at* WILLIE BOY, *who is in a world of his own.*
He leaves him and gets on the coach.)

EXT. VILLAGE GREEN. EARLY EVENING.
The area is now practically deserted.
We see GODFREY, MARJORIE *stands next to him. She has her hand*
in his. SANDRA *and* JULIE *are walking away. The* CONSTABLE *is*
on his bike and pedalling out of sight. Only a few paper wrappings,
and the marquee, remind one of the game.

INT/EXT. ON COACH. EARLY EVENING.
WILLIE BOY: (*To* LOUIS *in a quiet voice*) Everyone here?
LOUIS: Seems so.
(WILLIE BOY *passes by and goes to sit down by* YVETTE. *She*
slips her arm into her father's. LOUIS *starts up the engine. He*
puts on some light, but upbeat, reggae.)

EXT. VILLAGE GREEN. EARLY EVENING.
We have a medium shot of the coach pulling away from the village
green. In the houses that surround the place a few lights are now on.
There is nobody in the streets. After going a few yards the lights of
the coach snap on. The coach roars and bellows before it passes out
of frame.

EXT. VILLAGE GREEN. EARLY EVENING.
Only MARJORIE *and* GODFREY *in sight.* MARJORIE *is trying to*
take down the marquee by herself. It is a final gesture to rescue the
day. When it finally becomes clear to her that she cannot manage,
GODFREY *comes forward and takes her by the hand.*
GODFREY: Stop worrying. You did all you could short of
actually playing.

78

(*He starts to lead her away. Behind them the marquee blows like a sail in the wind.*)

MARJORIE: Do you think I should have volunteered to play?
(*GODFREY starts to laugh. We track them across the village green as they amble towards the early evening lights of Sneddington.*)

INT/EXT. ON COACH. EARLY EVENING.
The coach moves quickly down a country lane. The music plays on.
LOUIS *looks at his watch. Then he twists around and addresses everyone.*
LOUIS: I think we might make it back before the pub closes.
BOOTS: (*Gets out of his seat*) Okay, give me the map somebody.
(*They laugh. Some will sleep, others just think. They are all tired. The music plays on.*)

EXT. STREETS OF BRIXTON. NIGHT.
Under the closing titles we see the coach caught in the slow moving inner city traffic. It is raining lightly, and the glare of the street lights and the traffic lights is reflected in the puddles. They have returned to a familiar urban gloom.